Calling Cobber

Calling Cobber

Sheri Sinykin

Green
Bean
Books

Green Bean Books

First published in 2020 by Green Bean Books,
c/o Pen & Sword Books Ltd,
47 Church Street, Barnsley, S. Yorkshire, S70 2AS
www.greenbeanbooks.com

ISBN 978-1-78438-507-1
PJ Library ISBN 978-1-78438-511-8

Library of Congress Cataloging-in Publication Data available

Typeset by JCS Publishing Services Ltd, www.jcs-publishing.co.uk
Printed and bound in the UK by TJ International Ltd, Padstow,
Cornwall.

MIX
Paper from
responsible sources
FSC® C013056

Dedicated to a rare breed of Sinykin: women,
including my granddaughter Irina Mazel—my sixth
grandchild and the first girl born into our family in
sixty-seven years—and my daughters-in-love,
Debbie, Julia, and Cristina.

In memory of my paternal grandfather, Harry Cooper,
whose spirit helped me breathe life into Papa-Ben.

Note to Readers

Calling Cobber is set in 2000, exactly one year before the 9/11 attacks on America. It was a simpler time in many ways. The most common way to get internet access was through a frustrating dial-up telephone connection. People found home phones "busy" for a long time whenever people used the internet in those days. Cell phones were available, but they were bulky and not "smart."

In the 1980s and 1990s, CDs (compact discs) were popular, along with their disk-shaped personal music players and "boomboxes," which blared the music for everyone to hear. Recently, the silver plastic circles on which music has been recorded have become relics of the past.

YouTube was not invented until 2005, so Cobber would not have been able to learn magic tricks by watching videos, as you can today.

As you read, see if you can discover other ways times were different in the year 2000.

Chapter 1

"Okay, then. I'm going," Dad yelled from downstairs. "If you need anything, just call my cell."

Cobber tried to imagine dialing the number and saying simply, *Dad, could you come home now?* But he doubted his father would understand. "I'll be there as soon as I can," he'd say, annoyed. "Who do you think I'm doing all this work for?"

Now he listened for Dad's footsteps scuffing across the vinyl, the slam of the back door, the whir of the garage door opening and closing again. That creepy all-alone feeling settled over the house. It had been that way ever since Mom died six years ago, even when a babysitter had been there. His father had a way of sucking every normal sound out the door with him. Only strange creaks and groans remained.

Cobber snapped his shade down so his own reflection in the window wouldn't startle him. He stared at the telephone on his desk, wishing it would ring. His best friend, Boolkie, had promised to call after he'd finished helping out at

Nate's Place, his parents' downstairs deli. Cobber looked at his watch. Seven-thirty already. He'd call any minute now.

One by one, Cobber re-sharpened the three pencils he always laid neatly side by side on his desk. One for now. One for what if. One for just in case. Even though kids teased him, he did it at school, too. Somehow—he didn't know why—those perfectly sharpened pencils helped him feel better. They were something he could control. He placed them next to the middle-school talent show flyer, debating whether to throw it away or consider doing his magic act. He'd never before thought of performing in public. Teaching himself magic was his secret way of keeping connected to Mom, to something they both loved watching and had shared together. So, how could he stand up there in front of all those kids and parents? Surely everyone would remember what had happened in third grade. Three years wasn't *that* long ago.

The embarrassing memory surfaced without warning. Cobber walking to the front of the classroom, feeling his breakfast in his throat. Setting his diorama of a Hochunk Native American village on a low table in the front of the room. Licking his lips, breath quickening. Trying not to glance at his note cards. But when he looked up, twenty-seven pairs of eyes bored into his brain, paralyzing him. He swallowed hard, again and again. Bile rose, refusing to be swallowed. And then, all at once, the awfulness—spewing strawberry Pop-Tart and orange juice all over the table and his project. The funhouse-mirror laughing, the teacher's face pulled into a prune. He couldn't run, couldn't move. If only the floor had cracked open and devoured him whole!

Cobber shook free of the memory, focused on the present. No, there was no way he'd be able to perform his magic act, as much as he might be tempted. Then again, what kind of magician never wants to have an audience? How weird was that? Weird-weird, Boolkie would say.

Cobber wondered what he going to do until Boolkie called, until Dad got home. He could do what he wasn't supposed to do—try to contact Mom's spirit using her childhood game board that he'd tucked away in his closet. Or he could work on his new pencil-up-the-nose-and-out-the-ear magic trick in front of the mirror. That guy in the mirror—now *he* was the best audience! Cobber had just picked up a pencil, when the phone rang. "Hey, Boolkie—"

"Hallo? Hallo? Yacobe, can you hear me?"

"Papa-Ben? Is that you?" He felt a stab of guilt that he hadn't gone by to visit his great-grandfather lately. After Mom died, Dad's grandfather, Ben Kuper, had moved from New York City to Lake Tilton, Wisconsin, to be near them.

"Of course it is me. Who else would it be?"

"Ummm, Boolkie? Doing one of his imitations?"

Papa-Ben laughed. "Yes, well, I can assure you it is not Boolkie. So, how are you, Yacobe? Everything is fine at school, yes? You are reading those one thousand pages like you are supposed to?"

Cobber hesitated, not wanting to lie.

"Next time you come over, you will read to me, eh?"

"Okay, if you really want me to."

"So, is Larry there?"

"No, he went out to drop off a contract and get us some dinner."

"Ah, my grandson, the provider. The fisherman."

Cobber grunted, shook his head. They'd tried fishing a few times. Father-and-son bonding, Dad had called it. But they'd never caught anything. "Not hardly," Cobber said. "More like McDonald's or Taco Bell."

"What kind of dinner is that for a growing boy? And so late, too," Papa-Ben said. "You should come eat with me at the center. Have a square meal on a round plate, eh?"

"Good one, Papa-Ben. I wish I could."

"Well. I will talk to Larry. Maybe we can arrange it. You have him call me, eh?"

"Is … is everything okay?" Cobber asked.

"Oh sure. Fine. Just some little business thing. He is a good boy. He will take care of it."

Cobber grinned at Papa-Ben's calling his father a "good boy." Like Dad was a kid *his* age, even though he was forty-one. "Okay, I'll tell him. And I'll be by to see you soon. With Boolkie, all right?"

"Very good. I shall ask the ladies to make more cookies."

After Cobber hung up, he decided magic practice could wait. The talent show wasn't until late October, if he even decided to enter. Instead, he unzipped his backpack and took out his math homework. He loved all this fraction stuff. Mr. Kennard could give him five, seven, ten worksheets, and Cobber wouldn't care. Time flew when he looked at numbers. Unlike words. He was just finishing the last page when the phone rang again.

"Hallo, Yacobe, it is you?"

"Papa-Ben, what's wrong?"

"Psych!" Boolkie's distinctive snorty laugh gave him away. "Can't tell us apart, can you?"

Cobber clicked his tongue. "What took you so long to call?"

"Man, it was crazy busy! I can't believe it. Mondays are usually dead."

"Guess it's a good thing we didn't stop by."

"Your dad gone again?"

"Yep. Hey. Did you get your new cleats yet?"

"Um ..." Boolkie hesitated. "About soccer, man."

"Yeah?"

"I, um, I've gotta quit the team."

"Really?" A wave of relief washed through Cobber. Now he could quit, too. No more pretending he loved playing. Loved sitting on the bench, really. All that pressure. Pass it! Score! Defend the goal! No matter what position he tried, he always seemed to be letting someone down.

"You're not mad?"

"Mad? Why would I be mad? So, why are you quitting, anyway?"

"Well, that's the thing. See ..." Boolkie's voice trailed off. "It's just that ..."

"Jeez, spit it out, will you?"

"It's just that, well, I'm … I'm starting Hebrew school."

"Hebrew school?" Cobber blurted. "You're kidding, right?"

"No, really."

"Don't tell me you're getting bar mitzvah'd! We promised we wouldn't. That it just wasn't *us*. We shook on it. Remember?"

"Yeah, I remember. But you don't know how it is around here, now that Eli is having *his*—my parents acting so proud and everything. I caved, man. I couldn't help it. I'm sorry. I really am."

Cobber said nothing. What happened to all that talk two years ago about a bar mitzvah being stupid, a waste of money—and definitely *not* something they wanted to do? He tried to imagine Boolkie standing up there on the bimah, in charge of the whole service, celebrating being a Jewish man at thirteen. Ha! Some man, breaking a promise to his best friend.

"Come on, Cobber. Say something."

"I can't believe you're doing this. I should break a promise to you and see how *you* like it."

"Oh, man. It's not like that."

"Well, that's how it feels."

"I'm sorry." Boolkie sighed. "Look, it's just Tuesdays and Thursdays, is all. No biggie."

"You're gonna be in with all the little kids, you know, starting so late."

"Yeah, well. Maybe I can catch up. Or get a tutor. It's not like *you* couldn't come, too."

"No thanks."

"C'mon."

"No way. Not me. English is hard enough. *I'm* not gonna learn some weird language and stand up in front of a bunch of strangers and make a speech."

"They're not strangers, Cobber. Your whole family comes from, like, *every*where. You're the man!"

"Yeah? What family?"

For a long time, Boolkie said nothing. "Well. You can still go to soccer," he said at last. "Just because I'm quitting is no reason *you* have to."

Like I'd really want to stay without you. "Naw, I don't think so." Cobber twisted the phone's curly cord around his finger until it made his skin go white. He checked the three pencils to make sure they were still lined up, still nice and sharp. "Jeez, Boolkie, what am *I* supposed to do? Go to your house *without* you?"

"My mom wouldn't care."

"Yeah, well, I'd feel weird."

"You *always* feel weird. Come on, man."

"So, when do you start?"

"Tomorrow."

"Tomorrow?!" Cobber rocked back on his heels. Panic rocketed from his stomach to his throat.

"Sorry." Boolkie let the apology hang for a long moment. When Cobber said nothing, he finally asked, "If you don't go over to my place, what do you think you'll do? Go home?"

"Maybe. Or I'll visit Papa-Ben."

"But you don't *like* being home all by yourself," Boolkie reminded him.

Cobber rubbed his forehead, thinking. "Maybe I'll play with Mom's Ouija board. At least then I'd feel like *she* was with me."

"Wee-gee, schmee-gee. What in the world is that?"

Cobber tried to describe the mysterious brown game board with letters, numbers, and a few words written on it. "There's this flat, plastic triangle thingy. It has a window and you can see letters through it when it stops sliding around the board. All you do is put your fingertips on it and the spirits move it around to spell words or give you messages. It's cool."

"Spirits. Really." Boolkie sounded unconvinced.

"Yes, really. I swear Mom tells me stuff. Well, kind of. You have to fill in letters and guess sometimes."

"Okaaay," Boolkie said slowly. "So, this is for real? You're not kidding me?"

"I'm not the kidder. You are."

The statement hung between them for the longest time. Finally Boolkie found his voice again. "So, you're not mad at me?"

"Yes, I'm mad at you."

"But you'll get over it?"

Cobber wagged his head from side to side. He hoped he was making Boolkie squirm.

"Jacob," Boolkie said, using Cobber's hated real name. "Tell me we're cool, okay?"

Cobber hesitated.

"Hey, man, I have a *great* idea! Why don't you do your magic act in the talent show? I could help you with your patter. Your presentation. With my coaching, you couldn't help but be amazing!"

Good old Boolkie, trying to change the subject. "Just because I've shown *you* some stuff doesn't mean I'd want to do it in front of the whole school. Jeez, Boolk. You know I'd probably throw up again or have a heart attack." Still, Cobber toyed with the idea. It'd be a good way to hang out with Boolkie on the no-Hebrew days. But ... He shook his head. No way could he imagine himself not melting in fear in front of an audience. History had a way of repeating itself. Besides, if Dad had a thing about his using Mom's Ouija board, he was sure to be against him doing magic, too. His father wasn't a fan of strange stuff he couldn't explain or understand. Control, he understood, but not mystery. And magic required both. Besides, there was that thing he'd said, that arrow to Cobber's heart. But he wouldn't let himself dwell on that right now.

"Just think about it," Boolkie said. "You'd have almost two months to get ready."

"More like six weeks, but who's counting?"

"So, you'll do it?"

"I'm thinking, I'm *thinking*."

"Good enough! See you tomorrow then, right? Just say you're not mad anymore."

Cobber debated. Between that stupid talent show idea,

quitting soccer, and starting Hebrew, he thought he should make Boolkie more than uncomfortable. Really let him have it. Tell him off. *Some*thing. But how could he? What if Boolkie got even madder at *him*? Then where would he be? "Yeah. See you tomorrow," he said at last. "Like always." Always? Right. Since when did he visit Papa-Ben without Boolkie? Great. Just great. Once Papa-Ben knew why Boolkie wasn't with him, he'd be bugging Cobber about Hebrew school, too.

After he hung up the phone, Cobber locked his door, dimmed the lights, and hurried to get his mother's Ouija board from the closet. He really needed to feel that Mom was with him, especially now that Boolkie was bailing on him. Cobber placed his fingertips lightly on the plastic triangle. Mom's fingers must have rested there when she was a kid, too. "Mom?" he whispered. "Are you here?"

Shadows from three nightlights played on his bedroom walls. Too bad they weren't candles. But the one time he'd tried using *those*, Dad had sniffed them out in an instant. A real miracle, considering all the other things his father never seemed to notice—like it was a whole new century. He hadn't even bothered to hang up the 2000–2001 school year activity calendar Cobber had brought home.

"Please, Mom. Give me a sign."

He waited, holding his breath. The O on the window shade's pull-cord moved slowly from side to side, then spun in a full circle. *She's here!* His stomach fluttered at the thought. He *had* locked the door, hadn't he? Cobber glanced over to be sure. Couldn't let Dad catch him sitting in the dark, messing with her Ouija board again. He'd made that clear enough the last time. Cobber was pretty sure that Dad wouldn't like Cobber teaching himself magic either. That memory he'd been trying to suppress popped into his mind again. Cobber, Mom, and Dad all watching a TV special. Cobber and Mom had oohed and aahed over the magician, David Copperfield, who made a Lear jet completely disappear. The Great Wall of China, too. "That's incredible, isn't it, Larry?" Mom said, squeezing Cobber's hand.

Cobber squeezed back, caught up in the marvel and mystery of what he'd just seen. It made no sense, and yet he never wondered how or why. He simply bathed in the miracle of it.

"Ach," Dad had said. "Tom-fool trickery, that's what it is." With that, he slapped his knees, stood, and left the room. Mom had snuggled Cobber closer, as if to ward off the sting of Dad's words. But they'd found their mark.

Now Cobber stared at the little window in the plastic triangle, waiting for it to slide across the board. Maybe a real message from Mom would come through this time. She'd never quite made herself clear before. Still, he didn't lose hope that one of these days, her jumble of letters would actually make sense. He'd recorded them all in his notebook. The little blue spiral, in which he'd dated and written every letter, lay beside his left knee. At least she was *trying* to reach him. He felt certain of that.

Maybe she was waiting for a question.

Cobber thought hard. These first days of sixth grade were so confusing. A new school. Lots of teachers. Not to mention even *more* kids who looked at him like he was weird. A nothing. The kid who everyone said barfed in third grade while giving an oral report. Not someone they wanted to talk to.

"Mom," he whispered, "why don't I ... where do I ... fit in?"

His fingertips trembled. He pressed his lips together, concentrating on the two rows of letters and one row of numbers. They arched across the board beneath the three-legged plastic thing. At last the triangle began to move. It swung up and to the left. Finally, it stopped. B showed through its little window, then A, alongside. Now it was on the move again. The device paused on F, A, and M, before it finally slid off the board on "Good-bye."

Cobber opened his notebook, penciled in *September 11, 2000*, then *BAFAM*. What did it mean? He loved that Mom would try to contact him this way, but why did she have to be so mysterious? With a sigh, he put the Ouija board back in its hiding place under his sweaters in the closet, unlocked and opened his door, and turned the overhead light back on.

BAFAM. BAFAM. B. Bee. Be. A. Fam. Fam?

He pulled his mother's leather-bound dictionary from his bookshelf. BETH COHEN—her name as a kid when she'd won the book in a spelling bee—shone on the front in gold letters. He flipped to the F section and ran his finger along the column of FAM words. Fame. Familiar. Family.

Family.

He couldn't even *read* the word without something sticking in his throat and making his eyes go hot. If he ever had to write a "My Family by Jacob Stern" essay for school, he would have to make up something good. Something better than *I have a Dad who works all the time.* Period. Nothing else. Well, he had Papa-Ben, too. Cobber supposed his teacher might be interested to know Papa-Ben was ninety-nine and still in the independent-living part of the senior center. But it wasn't as if he lived with them or anything. It wasn't as if Cobber had a family like Boolkie's. The Bermans—now there was a *real* family for you. A mom who worked right below where she lived, so she could *be* there for her kids. A dad who trusted you to work with him when he needed help. And a big brother, so you weren't lonely, so you'd have someone to do stuff with.

All at once Mom's message came into focus. Cobber's eyes went wide. *Be a family!* Is that what Mom meant? But how?

Chapter 2

Cobber crunched into his taco, making as much noise and mess as possible. Maybe Dad would put his paper down and look at him. Crack a joke. Get on his case. You'd think he had gone all the way to Mars to get dinner, it took him so long. If only Cobber had ridden his bike to Papa-Ben's and eaten there—*any*thing, even cold cereal! At least Papa-Ben would have talked to him.

"Hey, Dad," he said at last. "Papa-Ben called."

His father lowered the newspaper. "Anything wrong?"

At first, Cobber thought Dad meant wrong with *him*—that he'd noticed. But no. They'd been talking about Papa-Ben. He shrugged. "He said it was some business thing."

Dad blotted his neatly trimmed circle of mustache-and-beard, checked his watch. "Well, too late to call him now. He's probably sleeping." Up went the newspaper again—the *Wall Street Journal* left over from work.

Cobber gritted his teeth. Don't say it. Don't annoy him. He warned you he'd had a bad day. But when he tried to eat instead, the taco had a hard time getting past the pile of words in his throat. "No, Dad," he said finally. "He's probably watching TV."

"Hmmm? What's that?" But the newspaper wall remained.

"I said he's probably watching TV. Papa-Ben *never* sleeps. Don't you know that?"

"Of course he sleeps. Don't be ridiculous. Finish up now. Don't you have homework to do?"

Cobber didn't bother to answer. That was just something Dad said—do your homework—because that was his job, what a father was supposed to say. And a son was supposed to do it, no questions asked. Never mind that he'd already finished it long ago. Dad wouldn't hear him anyway. The icemaker clunked out a few more cubes. Cobber choked down the rest of his cold taco and glared at Dad's newspaper. He imagined cutting a big hole in the page and sticking his face through it. Maybe *then* Dad would read *him* for a change and finally ask what was wrong.

Fat chance. Just tell him. Maybe he'll care. Argue. Try to talk you out of quitting soccer. Anything would be better than *this*. At last, Cobber knocked on the newspaper as if it were a door. "I need to tell you something," he said. "Something I decided."

"I thought you had homework." Dad set the paper aside, though, and finally looked at Cobber. Must have seen something different than the smiley photo-kid in that picture frame on his desk. "What is it, son?"

"Boolkie starts Hebrew tomorrow and—"

"You want to go with him? Great. Fine. If that's what you want, I'll—"

"It's not. And you can't make me, either."

"Who said anything about making you?" Dad sighed. "Honestly, Cobber, I don't understand you sometimes."

"*Some*times!" Cobber balled his taco wrappers. Maybe if Dad cared more, he'd *make* Cobber go. Like regular parents. Like Boolkie's. What? No way. He didn't *want* to go. He must be losing it. Dad was making him crazy.

"Well, explain it to me, then. I'm listening."

"With both ears?"

"And two hearing aids I might need someday."

Cobber's lips twitched to one side. "Boolkie's bailing on me, Dad," he said. "I can't believe he'd do that."

"He must have good reasons, son."

"Yeah? Take his side, why don't you! You *want* me to be bar mitzvah'd. Admit it!"

Dad blew out a long breath through pursed lips. "Look. You're mad at Boolkie. I get that. But you're not going to hook me into telling you what to do. Not about something like that."

"What about Sunday school?"

"That's different. I promised your mom."

"What about soccer?"

"Play. Quit. I don't care."

"Yeah, I know you don't," Cobber said.

"Coach doesn't play you anyway."

Cobber rolled his eyes. Thank goodness Dad had never

said *that* on the sidelines when he managed to make it to a game. "Yeah, well, I did quit. And Boolkie did, too."

"Fine. You coming home, then? Maybe you'll have time to do some chores around here."

"Chores! Are you kidding me?"

"What? Is Hebrew sounding better all the time?" Dad grinned.

"I ... can't."

"Can't or won't?"

Cobber considered the difference. He couldn't picture himself standing up in front of a crowd of people, talking *English*, let alone Hebrew. Couldn't imagine giving a speech. Having it *matter* so much that he'd put himself through it. Besides, if giving an oral report was any indication, he'd get sick all over the Torah. Disgrace himself for life. So much for *can't*. And there was no way he was going to pretend it was important to him, because it wasn't. The whole thing was commanded a squillion trillion years ago by a God he wasn't sure he even believed in. Nothing he felt in his heart.

"Tough question, huh?" Dad said.

"A bar mitzvah is just, I don't know, stupid."

"That's a pretty strong word."

"Well, it's just not *me*, okay? Look at all the time it takes. Years! And money. Don't forget how much those big fancy parties cost. And who would come, anyway? We hardly have any relatives. And ..." Cobber's gaze slid away from his father's. "And besides, Mom's not here." He rearranged the salt and pepper shakers just so, in the exact middle of the table.

Dad chewed on his bottom lip. For an instant, something clouded his eyes, a softening. Then it fled, leaving Iron Dad back in control. Like always.

"Anyways, who cares if I *don't* have a bar mitzvah?" Cobber said.

"If you think *I'm* going to force you, kiddo, you're wrong. Haven't I always said it's your decision?"

"Yeah, well, Boolkie changed *his* mind, didn't he?" Still, he wished he could leap up and hug Dad for not changing on him, too. But they didn't do that much ... hug. "I can still be Jewish, right? Isn't it like being white? A label? Something you just *are*?"

Dad scrubbed his face with both hands. "Yes, I suppose," he said at last. "For some of us, that's about all it is. But it can be more. A history, a community, a way of life."

"It's not *our* way of life, that's for sure," Cobber said.

"Look. I'm doing the best I can."

"You say that, but ..."

"You unhappy here? Huh? Wanna go live with the Bermans?"

Cobber swallowed hard, thought of his mother's Ouija board message. But even if that's what she meant, he couldn't say so to Dad. Couldn't hurt him, not after seeing that look in his eyes. And what if that wasn't what Mom meant at all? "No. I-I want to spend more time with Papa-Ben," he said. "Tuesdays and Thursdays. Regular-like."

Dad sucked in a breath. "Wow." He pressed his lips together. "I didn't see that coming, but I'll bet he'd like that. Wish I had more time to spend with him myself."

Well, *make* time. Yeah, right. If he couldn't make time for his own son, how was he going to come up with more for his grandfather? Cobber and Papa-Ben, they'd be orphans together. It beat being alone.

* * * *

Cobber waited that night for Dad to come up and tuck him in. He heard the phone ring late and then remembered … nothing. Just a warm, floating feeling. And then he was seated somewhere, people all around, hugging him without arms, lifting him up. Telling him without words that he belonged there, was one of them. He felt Mom beside him, too. But who were the others, those faceless people who welcomed him and kept him safe? Safe from what? He couldn't see beyond them to any danger that might lurk outside. But their music, the low murmur of their voices soothed his fears. *Jaaay-cob?* Someone calling. *Where are you? Come. You are safe now. You are home.*

"*JA*-cob!"

For a strange, wooly-headed moment, the sounds—*JAY*, harsh, insistent, and *cob*, so soft as to be almost lost—held no meaning for him. *Dad's* call, his *frustrated* call. Not Mom's. Had he just been dreaming about her two-note song, the way she slid from *JAY*, long and low, to a high, sustained *COB*—the sound she'd turned into Cobber, the only name he could wrap sense around?

"It's late! Get a move on up there!"

Cobber rolled out of bed and stumbled around for a moment, trying to wake up. He wished he could crawl back inside whatever he'd been dreaming. It beat sitting across the breakfast table from Dad and his newspaper. And it beat walking Boolkie to Hebrew school later, pretending he wasn't mad. Pretending he wasn't afraid of Boolkie not having time for him either.

* * * *

All the way from school to the temple, Cobber talked to Boolkie about every little thing—Boolkie's new video game, the soccer team without them, their new teachers, girls. The nervous chatter distracted him. It covered up the mantra in his head, the Big Thing: *This is it. The end of my regular old life with Boolkie … unless … unless we work together on my magic act for the talent show.* He rejected the thought. No way he was going to sign up for that. His stomach lurched at the very idea.

Finally, as they neared Temple Beth Shalom, Cobber cleared his throat and blurted, "Boolkie, are you sure you really want to do this? It's not too late to change your mind, you know. Just tell your parents how we … I mean, you … feel."

"It's not too late to change *your* mind either." A tuft of curly blond hair popped out above the headband of

Boolkie's backwards baseball cap. He stretched his putty face into a wide clownish grin.

Quit fooling around. For once in your life, be serious.

"Come on, Cobber. If you can't beat 'em, join 'em."

"No way. Forget it." *You can't make me, so stop trying.* Heat rose in Cobber's cheeks, despite an early autumn chill in the air. "I'm not going to Hebrew school, and I'm not getting bar mitzvah'd, and that's final." It wasn't enough that Papa-Ben was always on his case about this. Now he had to have Boolkie, too?

Boolkie clicked his tongue. "You're so stubborn sometimes. How bad can it be, going through it together?"

"Bad, okay?" How could he make Boolkie understand when he hardly understood all his reasons himself? "Think about it. Can you imagine me up there, leading a whole congregation? I can see the headlines now: 'Kid spews, desecrates the Torah.'"

"Stop it, will you? That was years ago. If Eli can do it, no reason you can't."

"You wanna bet?" So what if Boolkie's big brother—who wasn't exactly considered a brain at Lake Tilton Middle School—had made it to his last months of bar mitzvah training? That had nothing to do with Cobber. "Eli's got it easy. And so do you."

"What's that supposed to mean?"

Cobber kept walking. He didn't want to talk about it. Didn't want to turn this into a big fight. Why didn't Boolkie just go already and leave him alone?

"Cobber, I'm talking to you." Boolkie grabbed his arm. "What do you mean, so easy?"

"You guys with your perfect family, your perfect life." Cobber blinked hard against a sudden burning in his eyes.

"I never said we were perfect."

"Yeah, well, you are. I walk in your house and it's, like, no comparison." Images washed over him. What drifted out of Mrs. B's kitchen? Cinnamon apples cooking. Homemade gingersnaps, sometimes. Bowls of dried flowers in the living room smelled like vanilla and strawberries. Mr. B's sweet pipe tobacco hung in the air, even when he was downstairs at the deli. Dad smelled only of nothing-special deodorant and soap. And when he forgot to take the garbage out till Monday night, he sprayed Lysol everywhere to cover up the stink. Unlike the Sterns' white walls and boring old furniture, Boolkie's flat screamed with color—red walls and black trim, comfy new sofas great for gathering round with popcorn and watching TV. And the noise! That was the best part. Mrs. B singing to oldies cranked up to 43 on the stereo, then talking him and Boolkie into dancing with her. Crazy. Video games blaring from Eli's room, and Boolkie's, too. Cable news on nonstop in Mr. B's study. And talk talk talk. Yelling sometimes. But laughing, too. Cobber hated how quiet his own house was, like it had died, too, along with Mom.

"Hey." Boolkie nudged his arm. "You still talking to me or what?"

"Yeah. Barely. It just annoys me how lucky you are."

"Annoys *me* how pig-headed *you* are. Just come, already."

"No way. We're two years behind. You really think we can learn all the stuff we've already missed? *I* don't."

"Sure we can." Boolkie paused to readjust his cap. "Think of the party we'll have, Cobber. The *presents!*"

"Presents." Cobber shook his head. As if anyone could buy him what he really wanted.

"Man, you're beyond stubborn."

"Philip Berman," Cobber said, "just because I have my principles does *not* make me stubborn!" *Principles? I sound just like Dad.* But wasn't that what wanting to be true to yourself was? A principle?

"Principles, schminciples. And don't call me Philip unless *you* want to be called Jacob."

Jacob. He looked down, eyed his laces flicking against the sidewalk. His name, true. But really the name of a stranger, the grandfather Cobber had never known. One more thing that was missing from his life, from his memories even. "Just go on. Get out of here. I hope you hate it. I hope you hate every last minute."

"I will. I promise." Boolkie grinned and stopped walking. They'd reached the temple. Too soon.

"You and your promises. Just go." Cobber shoved his friend, wished he'd shoved harder. Really knocked him off balance.

Boolkie held up his hands. "Okay, okay. I'm going already. Wish me luck?"

"*Bad* luck." Cobber scowled.

Calling Cobber

"Nice." Boolkie rolled his eyes. "Tell Papa-Ben hi for me, and don't let him cream you at checkers."

He wished Boolkie would get mad at him. Leaving would be so much easier. Cobber kicked at a weed coming up through the sidewalk. Dumb thing just kept popping back, no matter what.

"If you're trying to make me hate you, Cobber," Boolkie said finally, "it's not gonna work. Come on, man. Be cool. Call you later?"

"Why? To tell me how great it was?"

"Hey. You never know. Or maybe I can work on you some more about the talent show." Boolkie shrugged, raised one eyebrow, then turned away.

Cobber watched him climb the wide wooden steps and disappear into the white clapboard building. Stupid temple. They should have left it a Methodist church, the way it used to be. No matter how they'd remodeled it over the years, it certainly couldn't compare with that awesome stone synagogue in Madison. If this place still had a cross on top and stained-glass windows of Jesus instead of the Tree of Life and Star of David, Cobber wouldn't be standing here right now, watching Boolkie walk away. Just up a few steps and down a hall. Along a whole new road without him. His nose tickled suddenly. He wriggled it from side to side. Still, the temple blurred. But it was his own fault he wasn't on that road, too. Maybe he *was* stubborn, just like Boolkie said. Maybe he *should* think about that talent show. At least then Boolkie would spend time with him again, preparing.

Chapter 3

Cobber finally crossed onto Johnson Street. Papa-Ben's modern retirement center at the corner of Sutter rose above the old gingerbread houses that surrounded it. The summer tourist season had officially ended the week before, on Labor Day. Now Lake Tilton seemed more like an Old West ghost town than The Place rich Illinois invaded each June. He could have dribbled a soccer ball all the way down Johnson, if he'd wanted to, and not bothered anyone. It was strange. Like living in two different cities without ever having to move.

"Hey, Cobber!"

He turned to see a car slowing alongside him. Joey from soccer was hanging out the back-seat window, waving. "You wanna ride to practice? Hop in!"

"Thanks, but I'm not going." He braced himself.

"You mean today—or ever?"

"Ever."

"No way! You really quit? But you've been a Cougar since second grade or something."

"I know," Cobber said, amazed that Joey really sounded disappointed. "Tell everybody I'm sorry, okay? I think my dad's gonna call Coach." For an instant, he let in a stab of guilt. Maybe he *was* letting them down. Maybe he did mean more to the team than he realized. But then he remembered Papa-Ben, how old he was—almost a *hundred*—and immediately felt better about his decision. There'd be other seasons for soccer, if he wanted to go back. Now that he thought about it, who knew how many more seasons his great-grandfather would have?

The kid shrugged, then waved again, and the car sped off. Cobber hiked up his backpack and hurried on. As the curving, multi-story retirement center loomed closer, an unexpected flutter, like moth wings, started up inside him. Usually, when he visited, Boolkie was with him. They'd just stop in, unexpected, and catch Papa-Ben watching *Judge Jeffrey* or some old Western. He was always happy to turn it off and sit around, playing cards or checkers and watching them eat all his cookies. And he was always there, in his room, alone. Always acted like they were some kind of gift God had sent him for no reason at all. Boolkie was great about teasing Papa-Ben and keeping the conversation going when things got too serious or too quiet. Cobber could always count on him to liven things up, when he himself ran out of stuff to say. What was he going to tell Papa-Ben today when he asked where Boolkie was?

Cobber sighed, imagining the conversation that was sure to follow if he told him the truth. Papa-Ben would be on him like brown sugar on peanut butter, asking why *he* wasn't starting Hebrew school, too. Cobber didn't want to get into it.

At the next intersection, he stopped to re-tie his shoe. To his left, down the hill, he caught a glimpse of Lake Tilton. When he stood again, he spotted Papa-Ben across the street, standing in front of the center, staring off at the lake, too. He was wearing his worn denim jacket and green Pioneer seed corn cap, leaning heavily on his cane. Its brass dog's head handle reflected a sliver of sunlight beneath his grip. What was he doing outside?

"Hey, Papa-Ben!" Cobber waved to get his attention, but he didn't seem to hear. After checking for traffic, Cobber rushed across. "Papa-Ben, hi. Whatcha looking at?"

He turned, blinked at Cobber, like a camera trying to take another picture. "Oh, Yacobe. There you are!" He cupped Cobber's cheek in his soft, withered hand, then kissed his forehead. The silver-gray stubble on his chin tickled Cobber's nose. "Thank God you are here now."

"I came straight from school," he said. Dad must have told Papa-Ben when to expect him. "I'm not late, am I?"

Papa-Ben pointed toward the lake. "I thought that was you down there, in that little boat. Do you see it?"

Cobber didn't, but he tried to, and as he scanned the dark surface, a memory swam up and started nibbling at him. He *did* see a boy, saw him at age five or six maybe, sitting in the middle of a little boat, Dad at the rear, his hand on the stick that directed the motor, and Papa-Ben in the pointy bow. He remembered how scared he'd felt, this huge darkness all around them, how he kept checking and rechecking the fasteners on his orange life jacket. What if he fell overboard?

"You've got to sit *still*, Cobber," Dad had said, more than once. "And stop asking so many questions. Of *course*, I won't let you drown. Of *course*, there are fish down there."

And so he'd tried harder to sit like Papa-Ben, to be this quiet rock who just *knew*, just *trusted*, that somewhere in all that blackness, there were fish. That they would come to their hooks if they were patient, if they believed, if they waited. And after a while, fear loosened its grip and disappeared little by little, like the morning mist. It left Cobber calmer and sort of connected to Dad and Papa-Ben. Left him with this *safe* feeling that they were all together in the same little boat—even though they didn't talk, didn't touch each other, just fished and hoped—and that even if the fish *didn't* come to them, they'd be okay.

Now he wondered whether Papa-Ben remembered, if he missed not going out more than a couple of times after that. Too much responsibility, Dad had said, taking a little kid *and* an old man out on the lake. And besides, things were really picking up with his work.

"No, it wasn't me," Cobber said finally, and heard the wistfulness in his voice. "Some other boy, I guess."

Papa-Ben glanced at his watch.

"What time did Dad tell you I'd be here, anyway?"

"Half past three. And, Yacobe, look here." He extended

his left wrist, showing Cobber the face of his ancient gold watch. Instead of lighted digits, it had three slender hands. The little knob on the side had to be twisted back and forth every day to make it run. Obviously, Papa-Ben hadn't wound it recently because the time read six o'clock.

"I think your watch stopped," Cobber said. "You want me to fix it when we get upstairs?"

"If you would. Please." Papa-Ben's glasses, the lenses all smudged with fingerprints, were inching down his nose. He eased them into place with the back of his free hand.

Cobber linked arms with him and they started off. He shortened his strides and slowed way down to make up for Papa-Ben's shuffling gait. Still, his great-grandfather amazed him. They'd have to throw him a huge party come April. The very idea of a century—a hundred birthdays, winters, springs—made his head spin when he thought about it.

"So, where is Boolkie today, eh?"

"He's, um, busy." Would he have to say more?

"Oh. Well. More cookies for us, then."

Cobber blew out a quick breath. "He said to say hi, though."

"A good boy, that Boolkie. Smart, too."

Cobber pursed his lips. Yeah, Boolkie was smart, all right. And if *Cobber* were smart, he'd keep his big mouth shut as long as he could about where Boolkie was.

At the entrance to the retirement center, Papa-Ben touched the handicapped access button with the tip of his cane. The door whooshed open. A couple of old ladies were cooing over the colorful little birds in the lobby's aviary. Cobber didn't recognize either of them, but he knew Papa-Ben had a whole fan club of residents who brought him cookies and magazines, even boxes of chocolate-covered cherries sometimes.

When he and Papa-Ben walked in, the women left the birds and started toward them. One pushed a walker that had a little seat and hand levers like on Cobber's bike. The other one was doing fine on her own. She grabbed up Papa-Ben's free hand.

"Well, Ben, *there* you are!" She seemed to be fighting with herself not to hug him. Cobber stared at her bluish hair, so thin that patches of pink scalp showed through. Thick lenses made her gray eyes huge. "Lordy, you had us all worried, going off like that, without telling a soul."

"My goodness, Clara, it's a free country." The walker-lady slouched over the handlebars. A gazillion brown-plastic combs anchored a fat gray braid on the top of her head. She lowered her chin and seemed to bat invisible eyelashes at Papa-Ben. "There's no law says a body has to stay in his room all the time, just because you want him to be there whenever *you* come a knockin'."

Cobber pressed his lips together to keep from grinning. The lady reminded him of Megan O'Brien, the biggest flirt in sixth grade. Megan would flirt with anybody—even him. He wondered whether Papa-Ben got as tongue-tied at all that attention as he did. Maybe so, because now he just stood there, saying nothing.

"Haven't I seen you before?" the lady with the braid asked. "Don't you usually come round here with a sweet little blond boy?"

"I, uh …" Cobber swallowed hard and stole a sideways glance at Papa-Ben, hoping he wouldn't ask again about Boolkie.

"You must be the grandson we've heard so much about." The Clara lady let go of Papa-Ben and pressed Cobber's hands between hers. They felt cold, her skin papery-thin. "Would you look at that head of hair! Dark, like my grandson Lucas. And such waves! Wasted on a boy, don't you—"

Papa-Ben cleared his throat, and the rattle of phlegm brought the woman's chatter to an abrupt halt. "This is my *great*-grandson. Yacobe Stern." Papa-Ben didn't introduce them—maybe he didn't know or remember their names. Or maybe he didn't care or think Cobber would.

"My name, it's Cobber, actually," he said, nodding politely to each of them. The women frowned at one another, as if he were speaking Martian. "Cobber Stern."

Papa-Ben grunted. "What kind of name is that? To me, you are Yacobe."

"Yes, but you're the only one I let get away with that."

"So, do you play Hearts, um, Cobber?" The lady with the braid giggled when she said his name. "Rummy? We are tryin' to set up a tournament and we need more players. We'll adopt you."

Cobber looked at Papa-Ben and hoped he wouldn't

volunteer him. Was pretty sure he wouldn't. They were the same that way. Loners, except for maybe one or two people they felt really okay with. The last thing he wanted was to be adopted by these nice old ladies.

"Adopted? No, I think not," Papa-Ben said, but a smile softened his otherwise serious expression. "We have to go now. We have work to do. Come, Yacobe."

Cobber gave a little wave, took his arm, and started toward the elevator. Suddenly, the toe of Papa-Ben's tennis shoe caught on *nothing*—just plain old carpet.

Cobber grabbed him hard and kept him from falling. But as he did, his heart seemed to sink down into his stomach, heading for his knees, like they were zooming up the tallest building in Chicago. He could hardly catch his breath. "Are you … okay?"

"It was nothing. Do not worry. But thank you, Yacobe." The elevator door opened, and they went in. Papa-Ben seemed fine now. He stood there tapping his fingers on the side rail, waiting, silent. That fisherman again.

Cobber stared at the neat rows of buttons—numbers— trying to calm himself. "So, what was that all about?" he asked finally. "I signed on for cookies and checkers. What *work* do we have to do?"

Papa-Ben closed one eye. The other one looked huge behind his glasses. A slow smile deepened the wrinkles in his cheeks.

"Tell me," Cobber begged.

Chapter 4

While Papa-Ben jiggled his key in the lock once, twice, three times, Cobber braced himself for the familiar slap of piney cleaning stuff left over from the morning staff lady. "You want me to help?" he asked finally.

"No, no. I almost have it." When the bolt slid back on his fifth attempt, Papa-Ben straightened, a slow grin pinking up his cheeks. "You see?" He kissed his fingers, then touched them gently to a narrow weathered copper-and-brass plaque mounted high on the right door jamb.

Cobber had never noticed it before. Usually when he visited, Papa-Ben was already inside. So what reason would he have for looking up when he knocked on the door? "What's that?" he asked.

"Do they teach you *nothing* at that Sunday school of yours?" Papa-Ben clicked his tongue. It sounded like his dentures were loose. "You do not know what a mezuzah is?"

A mezuzah. Oh yeah. Good old Sunday school. Every week the same thing—two boring hours of prayers and history he'd never remember. Unbelievable stories about seas parting and burning bushes speaking. Teachers should know better. Spice it up some. But mezuzahs, shoot. Someone had hung them all over the temple, outside each classroom door—ceramic ones that looked more like decorations than religious things. That, he *should* have remembered. "What I meant was, I've never seen you do that before. Kiss your fingers and stuff," he said finally.

"What you *really* mean, Yacobe, is that you never noticed before, eh?"

He sighed, nodded. For all he knew, they had one at *their* house he hadn't noticed before, either. He and Dad usually came and went through the garage door, not the front door. If they did have one there, it was next to invisible. And anyway, Dad wasn't a kisser—of decorations *or* people.

As soon as Papa-Ben pushed the door open, an awful new smell blasted Cobber square in the face. It stunk of sulfur and burnt rubber like a science experiment gone majorly wrong. "Eeew!" He dropped his backpack and shrugged out of his windbreaker. "Papa-Ben, what *is* that?"

"What?" His great-grandfather stripped his jacket off and hung it and his cap on the coat tree.

"That *smell*!" Cobber couldn't believe Papa-Ben just stood there, blinking from behind his smudged glasses as if nothing were wrong. That stench was covering up everything normal about his little apartment.

"What is the matter, Yacobe?"

"You can't *smell* that?" Papa-Ben shook his head, but Cobber's face was still puckered up as if he were sucking a lemon. Smoke drew him into the kitchen. Immediately, he saw the problem. A burner glowed red beneath an empty pot. Three, maybe four, eggs had exploded all over the place. "Oh no!" He turned the stove off and put the pot in the sink. When he twisted the water on full blast, steam hissed and rose in a cloud. But burnt pieces of shell still stuck to the bottom.

Papa-Ben inched up beside him. "Oh my *Gott*, Yacobe, what happened in here?" He made that same clicking sound between his teeth as he looked at the walls, the counter, the hood fan, splattered now with bits of shell and burnt egg.

"All the water boiled out. And why doesn't your smoke detector work? Jeez, Papa-Ben, you could have burned the whole place down!" The instant the words left his mouth, he wished he could reel them back in. Anyone could make a mistake like that. What good did yelling do? "When did you put these eggs on, anyway?" he asked, more calmly.

Papa-Ben shrugged. "I am not sure, Yacobe. Before I went down to look for you, eh?"

How long ago was *that*? Cobber sighed and set to work trying to sponge away the bits of egg. "Sorry I yelled. But you've got to be more careful, Papa-Ben, okay?" He squeezed his great-grandfather's hand and felt all his bones through his thin dry skin. "I'm only trying to keep you safe."

"Yes, I know. I am sorry, Yacobe. It will not happen again. I promise you that."

"Good."

"No need to tell Larry, then." A statement, not a question. Papa-Ben pushed his glasses up his nose.

Cobber hesitated. Maybe Dad would want to know. But what could he do now? It was over. Done with. Cobber had handled it just fine, even without Boolkie being there. His father had enough to worry about, showing all his fancy houses, closing his big deals, taking care of him. *He* was with Papa-Ben now, would be here regular, too. Like a job, almost. He'd watch out for him. "No," Cobber said finally. "No need at all."

"You promise?"

"I promise."

"Thank you, Yacobe." Papa-Ben avoided his eyes.

As quickly as he could, Cobber wiped up the egg and shell. He scanned the small apartment but didn't see any other mess around. The place looked as tidy as usual. The same old photographs lined the walls, the end tables, the bookshelf. The colorful blanket crocheted by Great-Grandma Dvosha—an *afghan*, Papa-Ben called it—draped neatly over the back of his scratchy plaid sofa. "So, what work do we have to do, anyway?"

"Oh, Yacobe, wait till you see!" Papa-Ben's eyes looked even bigger behind his thick glasses. "Larry came by before and—"

"Why was *he* here?" And what work did he leave behind? Sorting photocopies for some real estate meeting? Great.

"Sit, Yacobe." Papa-Ben pointed to his favorite green vinyl recliner, and Cobber obeyed. "I will show you."

He made his way to the drawn, beige drapes that hid his tiny balcony. With a great flourish, he tugged them open. Cobber drummed on his thighs, liking the effect, the drama. A brown paper sack, a wooden planter, and a plastic bag of dirt sat on the balcony alongside Papa-Ben's lounge chair. Cobber frowned. "What's all that?"

"Tulip bulbs. Larry says if we plant them now, they will bloom in the spring."

"Dad brought these? Are you kidding? Hey, maybe they'll come up in time for your birthday."

"God willing, I should live so long."

"Of course you will." Cobber's fingers itched. He looked around for something that needed straightening up. But Papa-Ben's coffee table was bare. "Don't even talk like that."

"Why not?" Papa-Ben shrugged and said something in Russian that sounded like "staryy ne molod."

"What does that mean?"

"Old is not young, *verstehst*?"

Cobber nodded, pretended he understood. But it made no sense. Obviously, old is not young. This entire subject was making him squirm.

Papa-Ben came up beside him and patted his shoulder. "Do not worry, Yacobe. That is God's job."

Easy for him to say. Where was God when Mom died?

"You must be hungry, eh, Yacobe? First, we eat. Then we work."

"What've you got?" *And don't say egg salad.* Boolkie would have said that out loud and, for him, Papa-Ben would have laughed. But Cobber worried he'd think *he* was making fun of him. "You relax. I can get it." He headed for the narrow kitchen.

"One of the ladies brought me mandelbrot, and we can have a little tea with our sugar." Papa-Ben laughed at his own joke.

Hey, it's Boolkie who shovels the sugar in, not me. But he bit his tongue. Didn't want Papa-Ben asking any more questions about where Boolkie was today, that was for sure. "I'll put the water on, okay?"

As he filled the kettle, he made a face at the blackened bottom of the soaking pot. Lucky something hadn't caught on fire. He shuddered at the thought. Better ask someone in the office to check on that smoke detector. Maybe the battery was dead. After turning the burner on again, he noticed a paper plate heaped high with finger-shaped cookies. Great. He'd had those before. Had practically broken a tooth and dislocated his jaw, they were so hard.

"Take care with the tea, Yacobe," Papa-Ben called from the table. "Mind you don't burn yourself."

He smiled at his great-grandfather taking care of *him*. "Don't worry. I won't."

When at last they were both seated around the little table, Cobber asked Papa-Ben for his watch and re-set it. "Remember to wind it, okay?" he said.

"I will. Thank you, Yacobe." Papa-Ben dunked a mandelbrot into his steaming cup and winked. "Go ahead. Try dipping. It is no sin to save your teeth."

Cobber grinned. "Why don't you just *tell* her chocolate chips are your favorite?"

"What, and hurt the poor woman's feelings? Now, *you*— you could tell her that, eh? Or Boolkie." Papa-Ben frowned, shook his head. "I forget where you said he is."

"I, uh—" Cobber touched the handle of his teacup, setting it at a perfect right angle and straightening his spoon. "I think he started taking a class."

"Oh, well. Maybe he will come another day."

"I hope so." Cobber took a sip of tea, drew his face up. At the heat, at what he hadn't told Papa-Ben about Boolkie, at the bitter taste it left. Maybe Boolkie wasn't the only one who needed sugar to make things go down easier. "Hey, Papa-Ben, next time you see that lady, point her out, okay? And never mind about Boolkie. *I'll* tell her about the chocolate chips."

Papa-Ben winked as he passed the sugar bowl. "Or oatmeal and raisin," he said. "That would be good, too. Come now. Eat. Then we will do the tulips."

* * * *

After Cobber had filled the wooden planter box, Papa-Ben stood over him, pointing with the tip of his cane. "Pack them in there now, Yacobe. Other way! The pointed side down."

Cobber looked closer at the bulb. Little root-like fibers stuck out of the fatter end. "I don't think so." If only Boolkie were here. He was a walking encyclopedia when it came to anything but math. "Aren't there any directions with these things?"

"We do not need directions. How hard can it be to plant flowers?"

Cobber shrugged. "If we're wrong, you know, they'll grow down, not up."

"Call Larry. He will know."

"I doubt it." When had Dad ever spent time planting flowers in his *own* yard? The few daffodils and red tulips that popped up and died quickly each spring were left over from Mom.

"Now, Yacobe. Let us have none of that. Larry knows everything." Papa-Ben nodded firmly. "He is a smart boy, my grandson. You call him, you will see."

"What's the use? I'll get his voice mail, that's what." Cobber set the bulb down, lining it up with the others, working to make all the pointy ends face up. "I can't believe he had time to come over here. He's so *busy* and all."

Papa-Ben clicked his tongue three times. "Do not talk that way about your father, Yacobe. He is carrying all the family on his shoulders, can you not see that?"

Cobber brushed a speck of dirt off his jeans. He should have known Papa-Ben would take Dad's side.

"You must try to understand, Yacobe. Do you remember that clown at the circus? The one with so many balls going up and down all the time?"

"The juggler? Yeah, so?" He looked up from the neat row of bulbs, satisfied he could do no more.

"The juggler, yes. That is your father. I am a ball. You are a ball. The people at his work are more balls. He is trying not to drop us."

Cobber smiled, picturing Dad juggling little round people. They looked like toy Weebles with better faces. Still, he made no move to go call.

"I am not fooling with you, Yacobe." Papa-Ben's unusually stern expression made Cobber wipe the grin off his face. "Call him."

"Fine. I'll be right back." Why did Dad have to bring those stupid tulip bulbs over, anyway? If it weren't for him, they'd be playing checkers or cards like they always did. Having fun. Not arguing about which way was up.

Dad's office phone went straight to voice mail. He picked up his cell on the first ring, though, as if he'd been waiting for a call. "Cobber? Is everything okay?"

He couldn't tell whether Dad's worry was for him or for Papa-Ben. "Yeah, except for those tulips," he said. "We can't decide which way to plant them."

"What do you mean, which way? Just put them in the dirt."

"It's not that easy. The bulbs aren't round, you know. One side's pointy and the other's not."

"Well, for Pete's sake. How should *I* know? Call somebody at Yung's, why don't you? That's where I got them."

"Okay." Cobber sighed.

"Is Papa-Ben all right?"

He remembered his promise not to tell about the

41

exploded eggs. But what about finding him downstairs, confused about the time? "I, uh, I guess he's okay. A little … I don't know. It's probably nothing."

"What? Tell me, son."

"I-I think maybe he's starting to forget stuff."

"What kind of stuff? He remembered I had to pay his rent."

"Never mind. It's no big deal." But the rotten egg smell still hanging in the air chided him. Maybe he *should* say something. He imagined Papa-Ben's face when Dad started in on him about what could have happened. Imagined how Papa-Ben would feel when he realized Cobber had broken his promise not to tell. Even *more* rotten. Like he couldn't trust anybody. No. There was no way he was going to do to Papa-Ben what Boolkie had done to him. "He forgot to wind his watch, okay? Jeez, Dad," he said. "It's not the end of the world."

Chapter 5

A brand-new air-freshener tree dangled from Dad's rearview mirror, filling the car with the nip of Sea-Breeze. The floor mat looked freshly vacuumed. "Da-ad," Cobber said, annoyed, "is *that* what took you so long? Another car wash?"

"That, and a last-minute call."

"Yeah, well, I was ready to give up on you and go eat dinner with Papa-Ben. I thought you forgot about me."

"Would I do that?"

Maybe. Cobber didn't answer. Instead, he stared out the window. Darkness was sneaking up earlier now. Soon the trees would be stripped of leaves, the lake covered with ice. Then Christmas decorations and baby Jesus scenes would erupt all over the place, reminding him at every corner that he didn't belong—not really—even in his own town.

"So, how did it go with Papa-Ben?" Dad asked finally.

"It would have gone better if you hadn't brought those stupid tulip bulbs over. The lady at Yung's said you can't put them in planters. They'll freeze."

"You're kidding. Your mom always—"

"Put them in the *ground*, Dad. Jeez."

"So, I made a mistake."

"Yeah, but *you* didn't have to deal with it. Papa-Ben got all upset. He acted like you'd given him a present and *I'd* taken it away." Cobber's cheeks burned. He glanced sideways at his father, but Dad's eyes were fixed on the road. "Dad? Did you hear me? It's not fair you made *me* look like the bad guy!"

"I'm sorry. That wasn't my intention."

"Yeah, well. Fat lot of good that does."

Dad blew out a long breath. He loosened his tie, the khaki-and-blue striped one Cobber had given him for his last birthday. Finally he was wearing it. "So what did you do with the tulips?"

"Mostly what the lady said. Put 'em in a bag in the fridge. But Papa-Ben made me plant some outside anyway. Like he didn't believe me." Cobber's stomach churned, remembering. He hated how stubborn Papa-Ben had acted, how sure he was right. Hated, too, how disappointed he'd be when those tulips didn't bloom come spring. If he lived that long. *God willing*, he lived that long, Papa-Ben had said.

God.

Riiiight. Cobber gritted his teeth. Did He even exist? What proof did people have, anyway? Maybe they just made Him up. And used Him as a stupid excuse to go around killing people who didn't see Him the same way they did. All he had to do was watch the news or the History Channel …

Dad's cell phone rang then. While his father took the call, Cobber hunkered down in his seat. His stomach rumbled, and he wished they'd stop at Nate's Place. Dad could wait for their food, and he'd run upstairs and talk to Boolkie. Find out how Hebrew school went. Maybe by then Boolkie would have come to his senses and decided not to go back. But from Dad's side of the conversation, it sounded like he had a new offer to write. Which meant ordering pizza and going straight home to wait for it.

Dad passed the lake on their left, then swung onto Main Street, heading for their subdivision to the west. Finally, he ended the call, speed-dialed Dr. Pepperoni's—how predictable he was!—and drove on for a while in silence. "Everything okay at school?" he asked at last.

"Fine."

"You sure?"

"Yes, I'm sure," Cobber snapped. But he wondered if Dad knew something he didn't. Maybe Mrs. Kelso had called about his first language arts assignment—a flop from sentence one. How could she expect him to write about "The Best Book I Read All Summer" when he hadn't read *any*?

"What's bugging you, anyway? Did something else happen at Papa-Ben's?"

"No." Nothing besides eggs boiling over and Papa-Ben getting worked up about those tulip bulbs and him running out of things to say because Dad was an hour late picking him up.

"Well, you could have fooled me." Dad turned up Sheridan Lane, hit the remote door opener, and pulled into the center of the two-car garage.

Cobber thought he heard the phone ringing and hurried inside, flinging his backpack from one shoulder to the kitchen floor. He grabbed the receiver the same moment the answering machine clicked on. "Hello? Hey, Boolkie, is that you?"

"Do I have the wrong number?" a woman's voice replied. "I'm looking for a Larry Stern?"

He tried to hide his irritation. Sure, Dad was trying to earn money for them, but why couldn't people just leave him alone sometimes? "That's my dad. I'll get him."

Dad took the call in his study. Business as usual. Cobber laid out plates, forks, and napkins, then raided the ceramic canister where Dad stashed loose change and a few bills. Hurry up! Get off the phone! He had to talk to Boolkie.

When the pizza finally came, Dad was still talking. Cobber answered the door and took the pizza, but something nagged at the back of his brain, something he was supposed to remember, and he hesitated before closing the door. A flash of color high on the door jamb caught his eye. A mezuzah! So they *did* have one. He stood on tiptoe to get a better look. Unlike the bluish metal of Papa-Ben's, this one was like the temple's—painted ceramic, with two raised stick figures under a canopy. He wondered when his parents had gotten it. Did Dad even remember it was there?

He poked his head into his father's study, pointing at the pizza, but Dad waved him away. So, fine. He'd eat by himself. Dropping the steaming box in the center of the table, he grabbed two slices, then sat in his usual chair— the one opposite Dad's and next to Mom's old one in the middle, closest to the stove. Her chair looked even emptier than usual tonight.

Cobber's nose tickled. He looked away, toward the window over the sink. At the little framed oval of wildflowers that still hung there. Blue as a robin's egg and papery-thin, they'd been pressed and saved by his mother. He knew the story, the hand-me-down memory, from Dad—where the flowers came from, what they meant. A backpacking trip in the Rockies, before he was born. Cobber imagined his parents camping up there, smoke and wind in their hair, not even dreaming of *him* yet. But when he searched his own memories of Mom and flowers, he came up with something different—her smiling at him like sunshine over the fistful of dandelions he'd brought her. That, and yellow dust on her nose from when she'd smelled them.

Cobber blinked quickly and looked away. Still, he couldn't stop thinking about her. So many questions. What would she have told him about that mezuzah? What would she think about his quitting soccer and visiting Papa-Ben instead? Would she be upset he wasn't going to have a bar mitzvah? Though he felt sure she'd applaud him teaching himself magic, would she want him to risk embarrassing himself in front of everyone at the talent show?

His mind raced to call back his last memory of her, to examine it for some kind of clue about what she'd say, how she'd feel. "Go get your jammies on, Cobber, and I'll be right up to tell you a story," she'd said. Stories. She had stories for everything. Except for why she never came up that night. Why he never heard her voice again. And now, six years later, he hated that he could barely remember the sound of it.

"Sorry about that," Dad said, finally joining him.

Cobber reeled himself back to the present. "What is it this time? Some dumb tenant who doesn't know how to change a light bulb? Or—no wait! Somebody calling to say she found her missing spoon in her garbage disposal and wants to apologize for saying your repair guy took it?"

Dad's laugh sounded more like a grunt. "That was last week. No, actually it's good news. Looks like this lady wants to make an offer on the Spangler place."

"Your new listing?"

Dad nodded.

"Cool. That was fast. What's that make? Two offers today?"

"Yep. We got lucky. The market stinks."

We. Like I had a hand in it, too. Cobber nudged the pizza closer to his father and watched him eat—crust first, then the pointy end, then the crust again. The silence between them stretched thin enough to break. At last he cleared his throat. "I-I was wondering about something," he said. "Our mezuzah. Has it always been there? Where did we get it, anyway?"

Dad's expression went blank for a moment. He blotted some sauce off his mustache. "Oh. Yeah." He looked sheepish. "It was a wedding gift, from one of your mom's bridesmaids, I think. We hung it the day we moved in."

"You forgot it was even there, didn't you?"

Rather than reply, Dad took another bite of pizza. "Why all the questions?" he asked at last.

"Papa-Ben *kisses* his. And we don't even notice ours."

"Why do you suppose that is?"

Cobber hated how logical and detached that sounded, like a teacher not a dad. He shrugged. "Maybe it's because he *loves* being Jewish and we ... we just *are*. Like it's not something we think about all the time."

"Interesting observation," Dad said. "Maybe you're saying he's religiously Jewish and we're only culturally Jewish. Does that make any sense?"

Cobber chewed on that, on the difference. "You mean like Megan O'Brien is religiously Catholic and culturally ... Irish?"

"Yeah. Something like that."

"What I can't figure out is why people change—why they suddenly get religion. Look at Boolkie." He almost spat his friend's name, the traitor. "He never *used* to care about being bar mitzvah'd."

Dad reached for another slice. "I guess with Eli going

through it now, the whole thing's become a lot more personal."

"Then again, maybe he just wants to be the big man for a day and get lots of presents." Cobber rearranged the remaining slices in the box until they formed a neat half. Still, his fingers itched for something else to do.

"Isn't that what *everyone* thinks?" Dad smiled.

"Not me!" Heat rushed to his cheeks. "All I'm saying is it's not a good enough reason for *me*, okay?" Why was he getting so worked up?

"Okay, okay." Dad raised his hands in surrender. "I'm not arguing with you, am I?"

Cobber shook his head.

"So? Look. All I ask is you go to Sunday school. Learn the basic prayers, a little history, some traditions. If you don't want to study Hebrew, don't want to be called up to the Torah or have a big party, that's *fine*, Cobber. It's your choice."

Cobber cocked his head, eyed Dad through squinty lids. Did he really mean all that? Or was it just words—blah, blah, blah—*anything* to keep the peace? How could he expect an eleven-year-old kid who wasn't even sure about God to decide something this big?

"For that matter, it's your choice how Jewish you want to be—if you even *want* to be Jewish, when you're older."

"Oh, right." Cobber couldn't say aloud what he was thinking—that sometimes *other* people decided who was Jewish.

"Why are you looking at me like that?" Dad asked. "What did I do?"

"Nothing," Cobber said, his jaw tight. *Put it all on me, why don't you?* "Nothing at all."

Chapter 6

When the school bus doors opened near the flagpole the next morning, Cobber saw Boolkie waiting for him at the curb. Why didn't he call? He said he would. He promised. Yeah, well, must have been a reason. Hear him out. Don't blow it. The important thing is, he's *here*. "Hey, Boolk! I thought you'd disowned me."

"Oh, man. Sorry about that. Eli was on the Internet. Some research thing that was due today. Mom wouldn't make him get off so I could use the phone."

"So?" The single word held all Cobber's hope, all his fear about Boolkie's reaction to Hebrew class.

"Sew buttons on your underwear!" Boolkie hooted.

"I'm serious."

"Really? I thought you were Cobber."

Sometimes he was *not* amusing. Cobber blew out a long breath and started into the school. The corridor rang with the sound of slamming locker doors, the babble of voices, the shuffle of feet.

Boolkie fell in step. "Okay, you want serious?"

Cobber nodded.

"Hebrew sucked. It was long and boring, and I hate making those hock-a-loogie sounds!"

"Those ... what?" Cobber bit back a grin.

"You know. Like in *CH*-anukah or l'*CH*-aim." Boolkie made a throat-clearing noise at the start of each word, practically spitting at Cobber. "It's so gross."

Cobber pretended to wipe his face. "You can say that again."

"It's so gross? Or l'*CH*—"

"No, don't!" Cobber laughed, held his hands in front of his eyes, backed away. Inside, though, he said *Yes!* He just *knew* Boolkie would hate it. "So, we're on for tomorrow? You want to come over—"

"And help you come up with an act? You changed your mind?"

Cobber hesitated. He hadn't really. But if that's what it would take to get Boolkie to quit ... "I don't know," he said finally. "Maybe."

"That's great, Cobber, but—" Boolkie hung his head. "You just *wish* I could quit."

"And you don't?"

"That's beside the point. I *can't* quit. I ... I promised Mom and Dad." He looked up at Cobber, something unreadable in his eyes.

What was that supposed to mean? Cobber frowned, trying to figure out what Boolkie might want from him. Some kind of favor? Like what? Changing his mind about

Hebrew school and going *with* him? "Oh, no, Boolkie. Not me. No way."

"How else am I going to make it through? Please, Cobber. You and me, we'd shape that class up in no time."

Cobber shook his head, glad he hadn't promised anyone *he'd* get bar mitzvah'd. If he was going to break a promise, he'd never have made it in the first place. "Sorry, Boolk."

They made their way against the crowd toward their lockers, not talking. Finally, Boolkie broke their silence. "Oh, well." He shrugged, plastered on a lopsided grin. "You can't blame a guy for trying."

"No," Cobber said, stopping at his locker. "I guess not." It surprised him that he really meant it. Hadn't he been trying, too?

* * * *

Their language arts teacher, Mrs. Kelso, reminded Cobber of a hummingbird. Tiny and nervous, she darted across the front of the room when she spoke, stopping only when someone's attention wandered. The fact that she was hovering over Cobber's desk now brought a sudden end to his doodling. He put his pencil down, lined it up with the other two, and looked up.

Mrs. Kelso gestured toward the back of the room. An older woman came forward then, down Cobber's aisle. She was wearing a sweeping, knee-length sleeveless jacket with colors that swirled like a kaleidoscope. Except for B.J. Kruse, she was the only black person in the room.

"Class! Settle down," Mrs. Kelso said. Her voice barely lifted above the din. "I mean it now. We have a visitor."

Megan O'Brien, sitting front row center, started a chorus of shushes. Mrs. Kelso beamed Megan her gratitude as the rest of the class quieted. Boolkie telegraphed Cobber a questioning look across the aisle. Cobber shrugged, fingering his pencils in turn.

"Today we are so fortunate to have B.J.'s aunt with us. Maya Harper is a real live author, class, and she's going to talk to us about writing. I'd like you to give her your complete attention now."

"I'm so glad Mrs. Kelso invited me to emerge from my little writing room to talk to you today. It can be a lonely business, writing, but I absolutely love it." As B.J.'s aunt droned on about how great it was to be a writer, Cobber tried hard not to doze off. He hadn't slept well, worrying about why Boolkie hadn't called. Now he wondered why anyone would want to spend all day, every day, in a little room, alone. Writing. *Reading* a whole book was challenge enough. He couldn't imagine himself ever wanting to *write* one. He glanced again across the aisle, but Boolkie was hanging onto the author's every word.

"Well, enough about me," she said at last. "More important is *you*. Did you know that each and every one of you has a special story to tell?"

Oh great. Cobber rubbed his forehead, braced himself for

what was sure to follow. *Telling* the story—in writing or out loud—right there on the spot. His heart kicked into overdrive. Why didn't she just ask for questions, let them clap for her, and go on her way? He wished he could get up to re-sharpen his pencils, but knew he'd have to walk right in front of B.J.'s aunt to reach the sharpener.

Mrs. Kelso wrote the word *HAIKU* on the blackboard, then:

> *5 syllables*
> *7 syllables*
> *5 syllables*

She drew a big box around that, then stepped aside.

Ms. Harper took it from there. "What I want you to do is tell me who you are in a haiku. Do you know your family history? Which special traditions does your family take part in? In short: Tell me about your heritage."

Cobber looked around, as if Boolkie and the other kids might throw him some clues about what she meant, what she expected.

"Don't go looking at your neighbor now," Ms. Harper said. "This is an inside job. Go deep. Be honest."

Cobber thought she was talking only to him and ducked his head, covering his burning earlobes with cool hands. *I'm different because I hate writing. And I'm special because ...* Nothing came, except that same old frustrated feeling of trying to make nothing equal more than zero. Which was a basic rule of math. Concrete. Logical. A right answer and a wrong.

Tom Phan piped up from the back of the room. "So, I am supposed to write about being Vietnamese, is that what you mean?"

"That would be splendid! Look to your history. What kind of an American are you?"

Easy for *her* to say. As a big deal author, she probably had loads of ideas and family stories. Cobber knew that Tom had taken a trip to Vietnam last summer to learn all about his Phan history; he could probably write his haiku in his sleep.

And Sophie's parents owned the French bakery in town! Everyone knew she could make the best croissants thanks to her great-great-grandfather's secret recipe. Even Boolkie had suddenly decided to get in touch with Judaism and have a bar mitzvah. Sure, Papa-Ben had immigrated from Russia, but he never talked about his life there ... so where did that leave Cobber?

"Class?" Mrs. Kelso snapped her fingers. "Let's see what you come up with in twenty minutes. If you have any questions, Ms. Harper and I will be here."

"Oooh, Mrs. Kelso." Megan waved her entire arm in the air. "Is this going to count?"

"Everything counts," Mrs. Kelso replied.

"For a grade, I mean."

Cobber held his breath. Maybe the haiku was just an exercise, a way to use up the rest of the period. As busywork went, coming up with seventeen syllables beat writing twenty vocabulary sentences any day.

"Let's put it this way," Mrs. Kelso said. "A good effort will help your grade, and no effort will definitely hurt it."

Cobber resigned himself to at least try. He ripped a sheet from his notebook. Its whiteness, its thin blue lines paralyzed him. Nothing came: no syllables, no words, no thoughts, even.

Meanwhile, Boolkie's pencil scritched annoyingly. Nonstop. Cobber glared at him, wishing he'd cool his enthusiasm. It was so distracting. Cobber peeked at his friend's paper. All he could see was the word *Jewish*. Leave it to Boolkie to feel okay writing about that; Cobber wished he could, but there was no way. Maybe someday but definitely not now. Finally, he headed for the pencil sharpener.

"There he goes again," one kid muttered.

Cobber ignored him and jammed one pencil after another into the sharpener, cranking the handle. The smell of graphite and shaved wood soothed him as much as the perfect points. He smiled to himself as he returned to his seat.

Mrs. Kelso flitted up and down the aisles, peeking at kids' papers. Finally, she paused beside Cobber. "Having trouble?" she whispered.

He nodded glumly.

"Don't worry about syllables," she suggested. "First brainstorm what you want to say."

I don't want to say anything.

"Just put down whatever's on your mind, Jacob." He

wished she'd call him Cobber, like everyone else did. Just *hearing* Jacob made him nervous, like she expected him to be some other kid he didn't know. "Remind yourself that there's no right or wrong, okay?"

Cobber nodded, picked up the center pencil, and straightened the other two. *Who am I? No right or wrong. Just begin. Let it come.* He closed his eyes. Frustration burned at the back of his brain. The wall clock's big black minute hand ticked like a time bomb.

Me? I am ____ ____ , he wrote at last.
No____ ____ ____ ____ ____ ____ .
I am ____ ____ ____ ____ .

He stared at the blanks and let his thoughts spin the way his stomach had been doing ever since Ms. Harper announced the assignment. He tried making lists of things he wasn't, lists of things he was or might be. Then blank by blank, he filled in the gaps.

Me? I am nothing.
No culture, no heritage.
I am just Cobber.

What would Mrs. Kelso say when she read *that*?

Chapter 7

"I don't want to lie to you," Cobber said to Papa-Ben the next day. "I … I just don't want to talk about it."

"Very good, Yacobe. Then you will tell me where Boolkie is when you are ready, yes? I can be patient." He eased into his green recliner, levered the footrest up, and settled back. If he'd shaved lately, he'd missed a bunch of whiskers. They were white, like his hair, but more stubborn-looking.

Cobber squirmed on the scratchy old sofa. What a chicken he was, not telling Papa-Ben the whole truth! Maybe he should just get it over with and hear The Lecture once and for all. "The thing is …" Cobber broke off and frowned. Somewhere water was running. Not a steady stream. Not a constant *drip-drip-drip*. But something in between—a cascading, tinkling sound that reminded him of the time he'd tried to flush his dirty underpants and, instead, made the toilet overflow. He bet even David Copperfield couldn't have made *that* mess disappear! "Be right back," he said, jumping up and racing to the bathroom.

Everything was in order there—the faucets off; the toilet, quiet; the floor, dry. Puzzled, he cocked his head and listened again. The sound seemed to be coming from somewhere *behind* the bathroom. The kitchen!

He charged through the living room, past Papa-Ben in his recliner. His great-grandfather struggled to sit upright, calling after him, "Yacobe, where is the fire? Slow down! Take care you don't fall and hurt yourself."

Cobber stopped abruptly in the entry to the narrow kitchen, sucking in his breath. Water was spilling like a mini-Niagara Falls over the edge of the sink. Already it was pooling on the vinyl floor. The little beige squares seemed to swim beneath the surface. He waded carefully to the sink and turned off the faucet. Next to a can of frozen orange juice, a dishrag had fallen in, stopping up the drain. Once he unclogged it, the water began a steady downward spiral.

"Papa-Ben!" he yelled over his shoulder. "Get some towels, will you? Lots of 'em. We've got a flood here."

"A what?"

"A flood. You know. Water all over the place?"

"Oh my *Gott*, Yacobe. Trouble, I do not need here. The super, he is going to be mad. I know it."

Cobber heard him shuffling toward the linen closet in the hall. Grabbing up a sponge, he tried to swish water away from the beige carpet that edged the kitchen. But it was no use. No matter how many towels Papa-Ben brought, the guy in the downstairs apartment was probably going to get rained on. What they really needed was one of those wet-vacs Dad sometimes used at his apartments. "Hey, Papa-Ben," he called, "I'm going to call Dad and—"

"No, please, Yacobe. Do not bother him. Whatever it is, we can handle it, yes?" But at the sight of the mess, Papa-Ben gasped and steadied himself against the wall. "Larry cannot know about this."

"Why not?"

"Just trust me, Yacobe. It is better he does not know."

Cobber took the few towels and flung them on the floor, as if they would really do the trick. "I'm not sure about that. I think we should—"

"Then call Boolkie, Yacobe. Quick! Before the super comes up here and I have trouble."

"You already have trouble. And … and I can't call Boolkie."

"Why not? He is your friend. He will bring his papa. You will see."

"He'd come if he could, but he can't. Not now." Cobber was throwing more than his own frustration into each slop of the towel. Dad should know about this. Why did Papa-Ben insist on keeping things from him? And if Mr. Berman came, wouldn't he tell Dad anyway? Fat chance he'd keep *this* a secret.

"But, Yacobe—" Papa-Ben's voice climbed—"you did not even—"

"He's at Hebrew school," Cobber blurted. There. He'd said it. Breathe. Just breathe.

"Did you say 'Hebrew school'?" Papa-Ben straightened,

inched toward Cobber, but did not leave the carpet. His frown turned his eyes into blue slits behind his glasses.

Cobber nodded. "He started on Tuesday. I-I didn't want to tell you because … well … I just didn't."

Papa-Ben grunted. "You did not tell me because you know *you* should be going there, too."

Be glad I'm going to Sunday school. Cobber bit back the words and slopped another soaking towel into the sink. "Can we talk about this later?"

"Oh, sure. We will talk. I promise you that, Yacobe."

Cobber swallowed hard and kept trying to wick up the flood in the kitchen. When he got nowhere, in desperation, he finally called the office and someone from housekeeping came up with that special vacuum. The whole time the man worked, Papa-Ben hovered over him, apologizing for "the trouble." After he left, Cobber wrung out the towels in the kitchen sink as best he could, hauled them to the bathroom, and draped them over the shower curtain rod. It bowed under the weight. He reminded Papa-Ben to make sure the staff washed them when they did his laundry.

"That I will do. Thank you, Yacobe."

"Yeah, well, I still think you should tell Dad about this," Cobber said.

"What he does not know cannot hurt him. Believe me, Yacobe. Look. The trouble is over, eh? Leave the man in peace."

With a sigh, Cobber returned to the sofa, and Papa-Ben followed. He hitched up his shiny slacks and lowered himself stiffly beside Cobber. "So. Why are you not going to Hebrew school with Boolkie, eh?" He angled his chin upward, as if daring Cobber to give him his best shot.

"Because I'd rather be here with you."

Papa-Ben raised one eyebrow, a white bird's nest above his wire glasses.

"And because, well, how can I learn Hebrew when I have enough trouble with English?"

"This, I do not believe. You are a bright boy, Yacobe."

"Maybe I *could* learn. Maybe you're right about that. But what's the point? I don't *feel* Jewish. Having a bar mitzvah would be a big act. A joke."

Papa-Ben winced at the word. "Bite your tongue, Yacobe. A mitzvah is a *good* thing. This is what it means, mitzvah: 'Doing what God commands.'"

"The only reason *I'd* do it would be to please you." His eyes met Papa-Ben's for an instant, then slid away.

"Not me, Yacobe. Please *God.*"

"But I don't *know* God," Cobber blurted. "I-I'm not like you, Papa-Ben. I'm different." *Just like that author-lady said.*

"Baloney!" Papa-Ben rubbed his nose, making it even redder. "I am Jewish. You are Jewish, eh? We are both the same."

"Then we are different *kinds* of Jewish. That's the only way I can explain it."

"A Jew is a Jew is a Jew, Yacobe. Bad men in history did not know one kind from another."

Cobber's breath rushed out as if Papa-Ben had just socked him in the stomach. He'd been afraid to speak that thought aloud the other day, when Dad said someday he might even decide *not* to be Jewish. "We're not talking about history now," he said. "We're talking about *me.*"

Papa-Ben shook his head. "It *is* the same thing," he insisted. "All Jews are *linked* by history. When we forget that, we do to ourselves what the bad guys could not. Why can you not see that?"

"I don't know. I just can't."

"You are a stubborn boy, Yacobe." Papa-Ben closed his eyes and tipped his face toward the ceiling. Maybe he was praying.

"Yeah, Boolkie said that, too."

"So? Stubborn you can fix, right? Just change your attitude, Yacobe. It is the only thing you *can* change, eh?"

Cobber thought about that, about things he wanted to change. Mom's death. Dad's working all the time. Boolkie's taking Hebrew. All stuff he couldn't change. But his attitude? How was he supposed to turn it off like a switch and flip on a new one?

"So?" Papa-Ben prodded.

Cobber sighed. "All I can say is I'll try," he said. "Really. I will."

* * * *

Sunday morning Dad dropped Cobber off in front of Temple Beth Shalom for the first day of the new term of Sunday school. Boolkie, sitting on the steps, jumped up to meet him. "So, when can we choose your magic tricks? It's awesome you changed your mind!"

"Is that what I did?"

"Man, you signed up! I was with you, remember?"

"I only did that so you'd stop bugging me. No way I'm actually going to do it." Cobber figured he could go through the motions and bail at the last moment. Meantime, it would give him and Boolkie a reason to hang out more. "You tell *me* when," he said. "You're the guy with the packed schedule." Though the sun made Cobber squint, the air held an unusual brisk snap, considering it was only mid-September.

"Fair point. Let me check with Mom, okay? I'll let you know."

They headed toward the front door. "Hey, Cobber, can you believe this? The beginning of the end, man! Next year, no more early Sundays. We'll be free."

"I'll believe it when I see it. They'll probably start having a *seventh* grade class just in time for *us*."

"Cheer up. What's two hours when you're with *me*?" Boolkie grinned.

Yes, Cobber thought. How would they have made it this far without each other? Boring Mrs. Bloom and her endless worksheets. Lopsided menorahs they'd made out of clay. Plastic Seder plates decorated with little-kid drawings. Boolkie's mom still *used* all that stuff, too, still kept it around—even the crayoned challah covering made out of a square of white sheet. Cobber remembered telling Boolkie once, when he was there for Sabbath dinner, how cool that was that she'd use *his* things, not fancy, real ones from the temple gift shop. The next time the Bermans had invited him, though, the cloth was gone, and he'd wondered why. Now, looking back, he supposed he'd embarrassed Boolkie to pieces by saying anything, though he hadn't meant to. And where were his own Sunday school projects? Probably buried in some box in the basement, if Dad had even thought to save them.

As they entered the building, an older lady with a helmet of stiff, ginger cookie-colored hair rushed toward them from the office. She waved at Cobber, then laid a hand on her chest, catching her breath. "You're related to Ben Kuper, aren't you?" she asked finally. "His grandson or nephew, maybe?"

"His *great*-grandson. Why?"

"I was just wondering whether he's been ill, dear. We missed him at services yesterday."

"He didn't go?"

"No. And you know Ben. Regular as Old Faithful. That's why I thought I'd ask."

"As far as I know, he's fine. I just saw him on Thursday."

The woman licked her lips. They were the color of those flowers that hung in baskets outside the deli, the kind some butterflies like. Almost purple. "Don't take this the wrong way, dear, but a lot can happen to a man his age in two days. I think you'd better have someone check on him."

"I-I will, definitely. Thanks."

"Tell him Fannie Spector asked about him, will you?"

Cobber nodded, and she disappeared again into the office. "You think I should go over there?"

"What, and cut Sunday school?" Boolkie smirked. "Papa-Ben's fine. They'd have called if he wasn't, right? Probably he was tired yesterday and slept in, that's all. Old Fannie's just using you to hit on him."

"She wouldn't be the first," Cobber muttered. "I don't know. You sure I shouldn't at least call?"

"Hey, they've got people who check on him. Don't sweat it."

Cobber tried to convince himself he was getting worked up over nothing. Of *course* Papa-Ben was all right. "Come on. Let's go find our room and ..." He was going to say *get this over with*, but remembered he was trying to change his attitude. "And, uh, see who's there."

The sixth graders met in a sunny classroom facing the street. Cobber and Boolkie took seats near the back.

A tall guy with shaggy dark-blond hair stood at the board, drawing some kind of time line. He was left-handed, and as he moved to his right, his left wrist kept smudging his handwriting. No doubt he was another university student, imported from the big city to teach them.

"Looks like more history," Cobber said.

"What did you expect?"

Cobber shrugged and read the events listed in the time line. Judah and the Maccabees. The Roman occupation. The rise of Christianity and Islam. The medieval period up to the Spanish Inquisition. Armies and fights and people on the run. Great action, all of it. "They should make video games of this stuff," he whispered. "It'd beat reading textbooks."

"Yeah. It'd be awesome!"

Other kids shuffled in—maybe ten altogether—and took seats closer to the front. Cobber guessed most of them went to the new east-side middle school, but a few probably came from as far away as Darien and Racine.

At last the teacher turned, cleared his throat, and introduced himself. He went on and on about what an exciting year he had planned, how they were going to read "Choose Your Own Adventure"-type books to bring history to life. After each one, they would have to write a report or do a project.

Cobber slumped in his desk. More reading! He couldn't believe it. How was he supposed to adjust his attitude to *that*?

Finally, the teacher took roll call, asking them to say their names, what they wanted to be called, and what they hoped to get out of this school year. Most kids gave kiss-up answers like "A better understanding of Judaism" or "A deeper appreciation for the lessons of the past." Then it was Boolkie's turn.

"My name's Philip Berman," he said, "but *puh-leeze* call me Boolkie."

"Like the sandwich roll with all the little onion flakes?"

"That's the one."

"Back east we call them bialys," the teacher said.

Boolkie only shrugged. "Doesn't exactly make as cool a nickname, does it?"

"I-I guess not." The teacher cleared his throat again. "And what are you looking forward to this year, Boolkie?"

"Um, finishing it?" Snickers broke out like hiccups around the room. Boolkie stood, removed his baseball cap with a sweeping gesture, and took a bow.

Cobber grinned, shook his head. Good old Boolkie. He was so great at thinking on his feet.

Ignoring the next introductions, Cobber stared out the window. A couple of kids on skateboards zipped past an old man on the sidewalk. Poor guy. They could have knocked him over. As it was, he dropped something blue. It lay at his feet. When he bent forward, stiff-backed, trying to retrieve it, Cobber raised up for a better look. The slump of the old man's shoulders, the careful way he moved … was it … could it be Papa-Ben?

Cobber jumped to his feet, raising his hand. "Sorry," he said to the teacher, "but I need to go. Bad." Without waiting for a reply, he sprinted for the door, kids giggling behind him.

Chapter 8

Cobber barreled past a bunch of little kids clinging to their parents' hands outside the sanctuary—waiting for kindergarten orientation no doubt.

"Jacob, where are you going?"

He turned to see the rabbi coming out of the office. "I-I think Papa-Ben's here." He pointed toward the door. "I'm afraid he might fall."

"I'll come with you."

By the time they reached Papa-Ben's side, a stranger had stopped and handed him a zippered blue velvet bag. With calm dignity, Papa-Ben brushed the wrinkles from his navy suit and straightened his skinny red-striped tie. A dark yarmulke fancied up with swirling gold threads covered the bald spot at the back of his head.

"Papa-Ben, you scared me! Thank goodness you're okay." Cobber flung his arms around his great-grandfather.

"My *Gott*, Yacobe." Papa-Ben coughed, his breath warm in Cobber's hair. "You are smothering me."

"Sorry." He stepped back. "What are you doing here?"

"Looks like you're dressed for services, Ben," Rabbi Brahms said, taking Papa-Ben's free arm.

"Yes. I never miss *Shabbat*."

Fannie Spector's concern about Papa-Ben's missing services echoed in Cobber's ears. Papa-Ben must have gotten his days mixed up. *Please don't embarrass him*—he flashed the rabbi a silent plea.

"Maybe you'd like to join the Breakfast Club in the social hall, Ben, while Jacob finishes Sunday school," the rabbi suggested. "There's bagels and cream cheese and lox, fresh from Nate's Place."

Papa-Ben frowned. "*Sunday* school?"

"Yeah, it's the first day." Cobber touched Papa-Ben's cane-arm and leaned closer. "I'd go to Breakfast Club, if I were you," he whispered. "I think Mrs. Spector's saving you a seat."

"Did she tell you that?" Papa-Ben raised his eyebrows.

"She said she missed you," Cobber answered truthfully. "If she didn't save one, I'm sure she'd *find* one."

"Maybe I should give it a try." Papa-Ben shrugged. "Something different, eh? Couldn't hurt."

"I'll be out by ten," Cobber said.

Papa-Ben nodded. The rabbi supported him all the way to the door of the social hall.

"Wait for me, okay?" Cobber called. "I'll walk you home."

Rabbi Brahms returned to Cobber, shaking his head. "He's an amazing guy, isn't he?"

"Yes. And stubborn." *Ha! Who's calling who stubborn?* "I was so afraid he was going to try to pick that thing up all by himself." Cobber met the rabbi's gaze. He had never noticed how direct and blue his eyes were, the blue of his mother's wildflowers.

"Ben just told me you come to visit him. Twice a week, he said." The rabbi smiled. "What a wonderful mitzvah, you know that, Jacob?"

The combination of his real name and the word *mitzvah* in the same sentence felt like a splash of cold water. He gaped up at Rabbi Brahms. "But I go when I should be here, at Hebrew school," he blurted.

"You *go*. That is the mitzvah, Jacob. Most kids wouldn't take the time or make that choice."

"I don't know. I can't explain it. It's just this feeling I have, like I *have* to, before something—" Cobber bit back the last, the final words, as if to say them might make them come true.

"I understand your fears, Jacob." The rabbi glanced about the entry hall. The kids and parents were still hanging around nearby. "Would you like to come talk in my office for a while?"

"And miss class?"

Rabbi Brahms shrugged. "It's up to you. I'm always here for you, Jacob. I want you to know that."

More choices. It wasn't as if he *wanted* to go back to class. Any other time, he would have jumped at having an excuse to skip. Actually, the rabbi was pretty easy to talk to. Maybe it *would* help to lay it all out for him—the bar mitzvah that wasn't and the whole disconnected feeling he had about being Jewish, about not fitting in. But then he thought of Boolkie, wondering what was wrong with Cobber, whether he'd gotten sick or something. "I-I think I should go back," he said at last.

The rabbi nodded. "Like I said. Any time you want to talk …"

"How about Tuesday, before I go see Papa-Ben?" The question popped out, surprising him as much as if he'd just belched.

"Tuesday it is. Say, three forty-five?"

* * * *

Tuesday after school, Boolkie was all set to go inside the temple, but Cobber hesitated outside the front door. What, exactly, was he going to say to the rabbi? Why had he said he would come?

"Come on, Cobber." Boolkie heaved the door open. "What's the matter? Chicken?" He worked his lips open and closed like a beak. Next thing you knew, he'd be flapping his elbows and squawking.

Cobber ducked inside before Boolkie could make a scene. "Well," he said, "have fun at Hebrew. Let me know if you can come over tomorrow. Hey, are you still having trouble with fractions? I thought of this really cool way to help you, using Legos."

"Nah, I'm good. It sounds interesting, though. Show it to Mr. Kennard, why don't you? He could use a better way to explain that stuff."

"Maybe I will." Cobber's brain raced to come up with another reason for Boolkie to come over. "I-I've been practicing some new magic tricks to show you."

"Really? Awesome!" Boolkie hesitated. "Oh, shoot. Tomorrow's Wednesday, right?" When Cobber nodded, he winced. "Oh, man. I can't. I've got to meet with a tutor."

"You? Ha! No way." Cobber tried to swallow his disappointment.

"A *Hebrew* tutor. And Mom's trying to get me one for Mondays, too. Man, I swear. Life as we know it is history."

"You mean, you're going to have Hebrew every day?" Cobber's voice rose. "Now we'll never get to see each other! There goes the talent show, I guess." Good. Now he'd have an excuse not to go through with it.

Boolkie shrugged miserably.

"I can't believe this, Boolk. I thought Moses freed the slaves!"

"Very funny."

"I wasn't trying to be." Cobber raked his fingers through his hair, felt how long and bushy it was getting. So, he needed a haircut. No big deal. He'd have plenty of time to get one now that Boolkie's life was planned out for the next century.

"Hey," Boolkie said, "if you can't beat 'em, join 'em, Cobber." He raised one eyebrow.

"No, I don't think so." Cobber wished he could do something with his hands. He felt like hauling off and slugging Boolkie—not that they'd ever really hit each other. Still, he made two fists. They hung, useless, at his sides. Well, what did he expect? That Boolkie could catch up on two missed years all by himself? *Adjust your attitude, man.* With a sigh, he opened his hands. "So, go already. You're going to be late."

"Don't be mad."

What was there to be mad about? Boolkie wasn't one to do things halfway. Cobber had to respect that in him. He was just feeling sorry for himself, that's all. *Another* attitude he ought to work on. Jeez. He'd be an old man by the time he got all his attitudes adjusted. "I'm not *mad*," he said at last and grinned as proof that he wasn't. "I'm Cobber."

"Riiight."

As soon as Boolkie had disappeared down the hall, Cobber headed for the office before he could lose his nerve about seeing the rabbi. The secretary announced him on the intercom, then ushered him into Rabbi Brahms's study.

He'd never been inside before, and found himself gawking at the rich wood bookcases that reached from floor to ceiling. Outside of the Lake Tilton library, he'd never seen a room so totally walled with books. A wheeled ladder in the far corner hung from the highest shelf. In addition to a sweeping desk topped with neat stacks of papers, the rabbi had a low gray sofa, two leather chairs, and an aquarium that burbled gently nearby. Several rainbow-colored fish wove lazily about the tank.

"I'm glad you came, Jacob." Rabbi Brahms rose from his desk. "Please. Have a seat."

Cobber sank into the sofa, as close to the fish as he could get. He hoped he'd catch their calm just by looking at them. Already his hands were sweaty. He rubbed them on his jeans. Who was supposed to start this little talk? He licked his lips, swallowed the pool of spit at the back of his throat.

"How did Ben do on the walk back to his place?" the rabbi asked, taking the nearest chair. He smelled of peppermint. "Did he fare okay?"

Cobber nodded. "He was pretty quiet, though. I think he was embarrassed—you know—about getting his days mixed up."

"You don't have to be *his* age to do that." Rabbi Brahms smiled. "Without my day planner, I'd do the same thing."

"Maybe." Cobber eased back against the sofa cushions and tried to relax. It wasn't as if he were in the *dentist's* office. "I think he *is* getting more forgetful, though." And then he found himself telling the rabbi all the stuff he'd noticed lately—the unwound watch, the exploded eggs, the forgotten can of orange juice in the sink that later overflowed. It felt good to tell *someone*. But now that he listed them aloud, they sounded pretty silly. Things that could happen to anybody. Why was he making them out to be such a big deal?

"I could make a call to the center about him."

"No, don't! Please. This is just between us, right? I promised Papa-Ben I wouldn't tell. He'd … he'd be so mad at me."

"Then you're not worried he might be a danger to himself?"

Cobber thought again about the smoke detector with its probably-dead dead battery, the burner Papa-Ben had forgotten to turn off. But his great-grandfather wouldn't make *those* mistakes twice. He shrugged one shoulder. "He seems okay when I'm with him," he said at last.

"I'm sure he is. But still, that must be a lot of responsibility for you."

"Not really. He takes care of me, and I take care of him. Like friends."

"But it's scary, isn't it? The thought of losing a friend?"

Cobber eyed him sharply. Surely the rabbi wasn't wiretapping their phone. "Are you talking about Papa-Ben—or Boolkie?"

"*Any* friend."

"There's lots of ways to lose them," Cobber said, thinking of Hebrew school, the thief. It wasn't as scary as thinking about Papa-Ben going away forever. Like Mom.

"Yes. That's true. And some ways are harder to understand than others."

He blinked at the rabbi, and, for a long moment, neither of them spoke. Cobber's heartbeat banged like a drum in his ears until he thought he would explode.

"You think we should … you want me to talk about … death—don't you?—on account of my mom and … and—" He broke off, unable to say Papa-Ben's name. "I'm not stupid, Rabbi Brahms. I mean, I know he's not going to live forever. It's just that, well, I'm not ready. I-I'm still missing Mom." He hugged himself to keep from flying apart.

"I know you are, Jacob. And from what I can see, your father is, too." The rabbi leaned closer, touched his arm. Cobber wondered why he'd say that. Dad never *acted* like he still missed her. Say her name and he was like Mr. Feel-Nothing. "When we love someone, we're never ready to let go," the rabbi said gently. "And yet we must."

"Why? Because God says so? And for that I'm supposed to love Him? How? You tell me *that*."

"God helps us be able to react to the blessings *and* the curses in our lives. He is our strength."

Cobber grunted. Yeah, right. Tell me another one.

The rabbi pressed on. "For everything there is a season, Jacob. Nothing stays the same. A bird learns how to fly. A child grows into an adult. Springtime buds become summer's leaves. Soon, in another few weeks here, they'll change colors and return to the earth to enrich the soil."

Cobber tried to breathe around the growing knot in his throat. He thought of his mother buried in the Jewish part of the old cemetery out on Rural Route 2. *Enriching the soil*, the rabbi said. But Cobber couldn't bear to think of her that way. Though he felt the rabbi's hand, still warm on his arm, he turned away. The little clock on the end table said it was already four. Shrugging off the rabbi's attempt to comfort him, he struggled free of the cushions.

"Thanks for trying to talk to me," he said, blinking quickly. "I guess I … I'm sorry I'm such a hopeless case."

"Now why would you think that?"

Cobber shrugged. "Maybe Boolkie's right. How can I expect to *feel* Jewish if I don't do the whole bar mitzvah thing?"

"Look, Jacob," the rabbi said, rising, too. "If you want to talk about bar mitzvahs—"

"I don't. Really." The walls of books seemed to be closing in, squeezing the breath from him. He backed toward the door, feeling awkward and, suddenly, as if he might jump out of his skin. "Papa-Ben's going to worry. I'm sorry, Rabbi Brahms. I've got to go."

Chapter 9

Cobber knocked and knocked on Papa-Ben's door. The rabbi's concern rang in his ears. Why wasn't Papa-Ben answering? What if he needed help? Racing downstairs, Cobber begged someone from the office to let him into the apartment. All the while, he pushed grim pictures from his mind. What would they find? And *then* what would they do?

The office-lady let him in and waited while he searched the few rooms. There was Papa-Ben, sleeping soundly in his bed. He seemed to have forgotten that Cobber was even coming.

Relieved and embarrassed to have jumped to the wrong conclusions, Cobber thanked the woman, then returned to help Papa-Ben get up. "You scared me to pieces," he said, smoothing Papa-Ben's hair back into place. He didn't like it sticking up like puffs of cotton candy, and knew Papa-Ben wouldn't, either.

But his great-grandfather only shrugged and said nothing.

The rabbi's questions swirled inside Cobber. All this forgetting. Shouldn't Dad know? Maybe Papa-Ben was okay keeping things secret, but Cobber wasn't so sure that *he* was anymore. He hated always waiting for the next bad thing. Surely Papa-Ben would let him out of his promise, if only he could find a way to ask.

Later, when they were enjoying their tea and Oreo cookies, Cobber tried to work up to the subject. "Are you sure you're okay, living alone here?" he asked.

"Of course. I am fine, Yacobe. God forbid an old man should take a nap! Is that a national emergency?"

Cobber shook his head, ate the middle out of his cookie.

"My *Gott*. You bust in here like the world is coming to an end. I should give you a key. Make it easy next time."

Cobber's throat tightened. He didn't want there to be a next time. Dad should be the one with the key, not him. *Too much responsibility.* Maybe the rabbi was right.

Cobber eyed the remaining cookies and couldn't help rearranging them on the plate. He made each one partly cover the next in perfect overlapping circles. There. Now change the subject. To something safer. He was a chicken, all right. Just like Boolkie said. "Hey, Papa-Ben, do you wanna help me with my family history project?" he asked. "It's for social studies *and* language arts."

Papa-Ben rubbed the silvery stubble on his chin. "I do not know, Yacobe. I am not so good with reading and writing. My eyes. These glasses." He managed a weak shrug. "Better you should ask Larry."

"Don't worry. I'll ask him, too. But we're supposed to *interview* relatives. All you have to do is talk."

"Just ... talk?" Papa-Ben wagged his head from side to side. "Well, sure. I can do that."

Cobber pulled his notebook from his backpack and lined his pencils up on the table. There. Better.

"So, how are you doing in school, Yacobe? Do you like your teacher?"

"In sixth grade you have lots of teachers," he stalled.

"And you are doing well?"

"In math, I am. But language arts could use some help." Cobber's shoulders rose and fell. "I'm trying my best."

"Then that is all you can do, eh?" Papa-Ben patted his hand.

Cobber riffled his brain for something else to talk about. "Did I tell you I signed up to be in the school talent show?"

"No, you did not."

"Boolkie sort of talked me into it. But I don't know. I'll probably back out."

"Why would you do that, Yacobe? You gave your word."

"Kind of. I didn't promise or anything," Cobber hedged.

"So what will you do?"

"Some magic tricks—maaaaybe."

"Hmm." Papa-Ben wagged his head from side to side. "I did not know I was sitting with the Great Yacoberto."

Cobber laughed. "You're not. All it takes is books and lots of practice in front of the mirror."

"How long have you been doing this ... this magic?"

Cobber shrugged. "I don't know. A few years, I guess. Ever since Mrs. Berman took us to a magic shop in Madison. A lot of tricks were really expensive, but she bought me this book. It was kind of like a how-to manual, using everyday stuff. She called it an early birthday present from Mom."

Birthday. He smiled, remembering his mother telling him how she and Mrs. Berman had celebrated their birthdays one year when he and Boolkie were just babies. "We went to the Overture Center. At night. By ourselves, Cobber. No husbands and no kids." Her eyes glistened. "Guess who we saw live. Just guess! David Copperfield! And now here I am, watching him on TV with you." Her excitement had been contagious. Though he was only five at the time, he still felt the awesome wonder and mystery of that show as if it had aired yesterday. No one could have known that Mom would die a month later. Embracing magic seemed a good way Cobber could still keep her close.

"If you want, Yacobe, you can practice on me, yes?"

Cobber shook free of the memory and nodded. What could go wrong with a small audience? "I'll try to remember to bring some tricks next time."

Papa-Ben slapped his knees, the matter decided. "So, let us talk about this family project of yours. Do you want to see pictures? Come. I will show you."

For the next couple of hours, Papa-Ben showed off his old photo albums. Cobber was almost afraid to touch them. The edges of the graying pages felt as crumbly as dry leaves. Few photos were labeled, but Papa-Ben could remember not only who they were of, but what everybody was doing when the picture was taken. Amazing. So how could he be losing his memory? It didn't make sense. All that other stuff—just honest mistakes. Dad would think Cobber was nuts if he mentioned them. Was it really worth breaking his promise to Papa-Ben?

"One more," Papa-Ben said. "The best for last."

Cobber studied the solemn wedding portrait of Papa-Ben and Great-Grandma Dvosha. Their hands were so close together, they were almost touching. Papa-Ben stared into the camera like he was afraid to blink. Or just plain scared to pieces. Great-Grandma looked way older than he did—maybe because she had already raised six brothers and sisters.

"God rest her soul," Papa-Ben said. "She suffered a lot in this life. I do not know how I have lived so long without her. What is it now—twenty years? Dvosha was—how do you say it?—the brains of the operation, eh?"

"I wish I knew her. And Grandma Rachel, too."

"Twelve years she is gone already, my sweet daughter Rachel. And my son, my Howard, more than that." Papa-Ben shook his head. His eyes shone. "A man should not have to bury his wife and children, Yacobe."

Already Dad had had to bury his wife. Cobber nodded, wondering all over again why Mom had to die so young. The rabbi talked about God giving strength, but from where Cobber stood, all God did was take people away—and for no reason *he* understood.

"You know what I am like, Yacobe? An old tree with no roots. Maybe God has forgotten me, eh?"

"I don't know, Papa-Ben," he said. "All this stuff about God, it's a mystery."

"Yes. You are right. And who are we to solve the mystery of God?"

Gently, Cobber closed the album. "We're nothing, Papa-Ben," he said. "And that's exactly what I told my teacher, too."

* * * *

When Cobber approached the retirement center after school on Thursday, he spotted Papa-Ben standing outside the entrance again, his back toward the street. The collar of his denim jacket was turned up against the wind. His seed corn cap perched at an awkward angle, half on, half off. He leaned heavily on his cane. Unlike the last time, though, he wasn't staring out at the lake, but rather at the building itself. Like something interesting was going on there.

"Hey, Papa-Ben!" Cobber quickened his step. He was excited to show Papa-Ben his new trick, how he could stick a pencil up his nose and make it seem to come out his ear.

But Papa-Ben didn't answer. Maybe he didn't hear.

Coming closer, Cobber heard him humming something. It sounded like that lullaby from the old country he used to hum when Cobber was young. He listened for a moment, remembering Papa-Ben sitting in a chair by his bed, waiting for him to fall asleep. Patient, like that old fisherman. At last, Cobber cleared his throat, but Papa-Ben did not react.

"Hey, Papa-Ben! It's me, Jacob." He tugged on his sleeve.

"No! Get away!" Papa-Ben turned, raising his cane as if to strike Cobber. His face was drawn up in fear, but then it softened. "Yacobe! What are you doing, sneaking up on your old Papa-Ben?"

"I wasn't sneaking. You just didn't hear me."

"Don't give me none of your baloney, Yacobe. There is nothing wrong with my ears."

Cobber sighed. How could Papa-Ben explain standing there, staring off like he was a million miles away? Maybe he *was* getting that old-timer's disease. Dad really should know, shouldn't he? Get him checked out? Cobber watched Papa-Ben closely all the way to the apartment.

"Why didn't you wait for me in here?" he said finally. "It's cold outside."

"Not so cold." Papa-Ben eased into his recliner.

This was crazy, Papa-Ben almost hitting him. Things had gone far enough. Today, he thought. Today he would work up the courage to tell Papa-Ben that one of them needed to let Dad know.

"So, Yacobe, come sit. Tell me about school. Did you decide what tricks you are going to do for the show? How is your reading and writing? Better?"

"Actually, yes!" For once, Cobber brightened at the mention of his worst subject. "Just wait till you see what I got on my haiku." Jumping up, he unzipped his backpack, pulled the assignment from his language arts folder, and handed it to Papa-Ben. An A in bright red ink blazed from the page.

"Ah, what is this, Yacobe? A paper with no numbers and a good mark, yes?"

Cobber nodded, and when Papa-Ben smiled, his eyes almost disappeared into the wrinkles behind his glasses. His spicy aftershave tweaked Cobber's nose in a way his knobbly fingers couldn't anymore.

"Wonderful! Wonderful!"

Cobber's cheeks went hot at all the fuss Papa-Ben was making. But he had to admit that it was one thing he missed, now that he went home some days to an empty house, instead of to Boolkie's. Mrs. Berman was a great one for making Cobber feel as special as her own boys. And trying to contact Mom with the Ouija board wasn't the same thing. Papa-Ben handed back the paper.

"Wait," Cobber said. "Aren't you going to read it?"

"It will sound better in your voice, eh, Yacobe?"

"But I *like* your accent."

"No. You read." A snap of Papa-Ben's fingers made it an order.

"Okay, okay already." With a sigh, he leaned over Papa-Ben's shoulder and began to read:

Me? I am nothing.
No culture, no heritage.
I am just Cobber.

His voice surprised him by squeaking at the end. It sounded like he'd used a question mark instead of a period.

"No … culture? What about being a Jew? Is that not important?" Papa-Ben tried to turn around in his recliner. The squeal of its vinyl covering seemed to scold Cobber, too. "Come around here, Yacobe. Do not make me hurt my back."

He slunk around in front, avoiding Papa-Ben's eyes.

"So. For *this* the teacher gives you a high mark?"

Cobber's excitement over his extra credit points leaked away like air from an old balloon. "I answered the question," he said. "It-It's hard to say who you are in only seventeen syllables. There isn't room to say *everything* about me."

"There is a big difference between saying everything and saying you are nothing," Papa-Ben said, too quietly. "What did Boolkie write, eh?"

"How should I know?" Cobber played with his fingers. He didn't have to clue Papa-Ben in, did he? Just because Boolkie was taking Hebrew didn't mean he was Mr. Super-Jew, no matter what his stupid haiku said. He and his family even worked on Saturdays. The Sabbath, for Pete's sake! And why didn't they keep kosher? Maybe the Bermans were better Jews than he and Dad were, but they sure weren't perfect. Cobber wondered why he'd never realized that before.

Papa-Ben looked like he was going to say something, then changed his mind. His lips snapped together and stayed there, firmly clamped.

"Don't be that way," Cobber pleaded. "You know how hard I've been trying to pull my language arts grade up. I thought you'd be glad for me. Proud, even."

"So, it matters what *I* think?"

"Of course!"

"Then why do you not study Hebrew with Boolkie, eh? Why can I not be proud at your bar mitzvah?"

Cobber sighed. Not this again. Why couldn't Papa-Ben just let it go? Or why couldn't *he* cave in and just do it? Stubborn times two, that's why.

"Maybe I am the nobody, Yacobe," Papa-Ben said at last. "I cannot even make you feel how special you are, being Jewish. This faith I have … this tie … You see? I cannot even find the words." Papa-Ben rubbed his nose with the back of his hand. At last he removed his glasses and wiped them on his soft flannel shirt. Then he put them on again. "This, I do not understand. I try and I try, and still I fail you. Maybe, I am just an old fool."

"You aren't a fool," Cobber said.

"But I *am* old, eh?" Papa-Ben's soft chuckle sounded strange, like a hiccup, almost. His lopsided smile made Cobber's stomach go tight.

"It's not that. It's just …" Cobber struggled to find the right words. "I'm worried about you, Papa-Ben. Why don't you want Dad to know you've been forgetting stuff?"

"You promised you would not tell him, eh?"

"I know. I did. But I don't get why. I think maybe we should—"

"I do not want to go to a nursing home, Yacobe," Papa-Ben blurted. "This is why. Do you understand? I like my place. My things. My friends here. I am fine."

"Dad wouldn't make you go there." But even as Cobber said the words, he suspected they weren't true. If Papa-Ben wasn't safe living on his own, what other choice would Dad have? "But what if … what if something happened and he *had* to? Would that really be so terrible?"

Papa-Ben's eyes welled, and he looked away. At last a strangled sob broke through his tight silence.

That sound turned to mush all Cobber's good reasons for telling. He couldn't bear it. "Okay, okay," he said. "I won't say anything. For now. But you've got to promise to be careful. *Extra* careful."

"I promise, Yacobe. You have my word."

When had Papa-Ben ever lied? "Well, okay then. My lips are sealed." He pretended to lock them and handed Papa-Ben an imaginary key.

His great-grandfather caught his hand and pressed it to his lips. "You are a good boy, Yacobe," he said. "God bless you, eh?"

Cobber cringed at the words. So what if God blessed him? Dad was sure to be mad when he found out they'd both been keeping stuff from him. He only hoped Papa-Ben kept up his end of the deal and didn't do anything stupid.

Chapter 10

Chill. Papa-Ben's fine. Think of all those photos he remembered. You're doing the right thing. Keeping your promise. And he'll keep his. Cobber shoveled down dinner, not minding for once that Dad was reading the paper. Too much conversation about his visit with Papa-Ben and he might let something slip.

Dad left soon after to show a farmhouse out in the country to some new clients. Cobber flipped the TV on and surfed through the channels. Any minute Boolkie would be calling for help on their math homework. Fractions. He had promised to call once he finished up downstairs, refilling the salt and pepper shakers in the deli. Cobber still wished Boolkie would let him use Legos to teach him fractions. Everything would make so much more sense, and right away.

While he waited, he supposed he *should* be doing his reading for language arts—a biography of his own choice. Maybe Harry Houdini and all his incredible magic escapes would hold his attention. Not that he'd started the book yet.

But he would. Soon. He just needed his full concentration and no interruptions. Instead, he practiced his Jumping Jacks card trick in front of the downstairs bathroom mirror. The marble vanity made a great magician's table, and his reflection was more encouraging than a real audience would be. Of that, he felt certain.

At last the phone rang. "Yacobe? You are there?"

He grinned. Good old Boolkie and his Papa-Ben imitation. Taking the downstairs cordless phone over to the couch, he flopped on his back. "Yeah, yeah, it's me," he said. "Who else would it be?" He put his feet on the armrest, as long as Dad wasn't there to bug him about still having his shoes on. Knowing Boolkie, this could take a while. "Boolk? You still there?"

An odd, hiccupping sound was the only reply.

"Stop kidding around, okay? I know it's you."

"Get … Larry." The voice sounded strange—faraway, but kind of choking, too.

Cobber hesitated. Since when did Boolkie call Dad Larry? "He's got a showing. Why do you want to …? Boolkie? Is that you? You sound weird."

"Get … help."

Cobber rocketed off the couch. A knot tightened in his throat, making it hard to speak, to breathe even. "Papa-Ben? It's *you*, isn't it? Tell me what's wrong!"

"Yacobe, help! Something … I do not know … dizzy …" His voice trailed off. Cobber thought he heard a thump in the background.

The line was still open, though, and he had to press the disconnect button a bunch of times. Finally, he got a dial tone and flew from the family room to the kitchen, punching nine-one-one on the way. What was Papa-Ben's address? He fumbled through the drawer for Dad's address book, flipped to the K section. Why wasn't *Ben Kuper* in there? Maybe he was under P, for Papa-Ben.

A woman's voice, all stiff and businesslike, came on the line.

"Something's wrong with my great-grandpa," he blurted. "He just called. Sounded funny. Said he was dizzy, and—I don't know—but I think maybe he fell."

The nine-one-one lady's tone changed, turned as sweet and smooth as melted chocolate. "Calm down now. That a boy. Where *is* your grandpa?"

His fingers hurt from squeezing the phone so hard. "I can't remember the address—the numbers, I mean—but he's in that retirement center at the corner of Sutter and Johnson. No, not the nursing home part. The apartments. Ben Kuper. Second floor. First door on the right. Two-oh-one, I think."

She asked Cobber's name, address, some other stuff—was he alone and where his parents were. He gave her the short version, leaving out the part about Mom. Why did she have to know *his* life story? *Just help Papa-Ben*, his mind screamed.

"How old are you, Jacob? Do you have a neighbor who could come over and stay with you?"

"I'm almost twelve, okay? I'm fine," he lied. "Just tell them to hurry, please?"

She told him to wait where he was, and he promised he would, only his fingers were crossed. The minute he hung up, he dialed Dad's cell phone.

"Whoa! Slow down. I can't understand you."

Cobber took a deep breath, tried again. "I just called nine-one-one. No, not for me. For Papa-Ben. Something's really wrong. He said he was dizzy, and—I'm not sure—it sounded like he fell."

Dad took in a sharp breath. "You did the right thing. I'm on my way over there. You stay put in case—"

Cobber hung up before Dad could finish. There was no way he was going to stay put. He'd take his bike; the ride was mostly downhill. Maybe he'd even beat Dad to Papa-Ben's. Wasn't he way out in the boonies somewhere, looking at that farmhouse?

He grabbed his jacket and bike helmet, then streaked down the driveway. His pulse thumped in time with his churning legs. "Please let Papa-Ben be all right," he whispered over and over to the fall night sky and whatever lay beyond. God, maybe. God, he hoped. *This* could be God's blessing—saving Papa-Ben.

Just save him, God, and I promise I'll start believing in you.

As he pedaled madly toward the retirement center, his mind locked on Papa-Ben reaching out to him on the phone. How much time had he lost, thinking it was

Boolkie? If only Boolkie wasn't always kidding around! A chill wind sliced off the lake. He huddled lower over his handlebars, caring only about Papa-Ben. At last, he rounded the final bend.

Flashing lights from a waiting ambulance bounced off the windows that faced the center's parking lot. Good. They were already there. Chucking his bike in the bushes, not bothering to lock it, he raced upstairs.

Papa-Ben's door was ajar. Cobber pushed past a couple of the residents, past blue-uniformed paramedics who were hovering around Papa-Ben, fastening lines and checking numbers on blinking screens. Papa-Ben lay, gray and still, on the floor. His silvery hair, usually slicked back with smelly stuff, stuck out wild as a scream.

Cobber slunk back into the corner, and, in a heartbeat, felt himself shrinking from almost twelve years old to five, to the night he woke up wanting Mommy and found all those strange men in the house. Heard them talking low. Saw Dad fold over and over on himself, not seeing Cobber at all. No! He couldn't think about that now. He *wouldn't*. He had to be a big boy, be strong. He hugged himself, trying to stop his sudden shaking, and crouched behind Papa-Ben's recliner—behind the colored circles of afghan draped over the headrest. No one must see him hiding and make him leave.

He peeked around the armrest. Papa-Ben just lay there. His lips were the color of raw chicken livers. Cobber's mouth began to sweat, as if a tub of the gross-looking things was sitting in his stomach, ready to come up. Someone had put an oxygen mask over Papa-Ben's face. It clouded up with his breath. Good. He was still alive.

"Any idea what meds he's on?" someone else said.

Dad could answer those questions. Cobber wished he knew how far away that farmhouse was. Shouldn't Dad be here by now?

One of the paramedics disappeared into the little kitchen and returned with a couple of prescription bottles. "Here—" he pushed them at his partner—"check these. Empty, both of them. Just laying there on the counter, caps off."

Cobber hadn't realized he'd been holding his breath until it rushed out all at once. "That *can't* be! He wouldn't *do* that!" Lunging toward them, he could see in the paramedics' eyes, in the way they flinched, that he'd startled them.

The blue-haired Clara lady he'd met downstairs emerged from the group of onlookers. "He's the man's great-grandson. I'll take care of him." With her slender arm, she wrapped the smell of ripe lemons around him, then led him aside, into the kitchen. "Is there someone I should call for you, dear?"

"Dad's on his way. Supposedly."

"Come then. Let me fix you something."

"I'm not hungry," Cobber said, but realized that he *was* shivering and suddenly bone-cold. Tea. Tea would be good. He scanned the stretch of counter beside the sink, past the opened package of Oreos they'd eaten earlier, to where Papa-Ben usually kept a box of tea bags. Instead, he saw

Papa-Ben's colored plastic pill container. Morning, noon, dinner, bedtime. Four lids gaped open. Half a glass of water stood nearby, along with a piece of notebook paper.

When he picked it up, the stupid haiku from school swam before his eyes. He couldn't focus. Couldn't think of anything but the bad feelings it had made between him and Papa-Ben. *Still I fail you*, he'd said. *Maybe I am just an old fool.* Cobber shuddered, remembering. But everything had been okay—hadn't it?—by the time he went home. Yes. He was sure of it. Papa-Ben had even wanted to *keep* the stupid haiku. Now he set it aside, wishing he'd never shown it to Papa-Ben and upset him. So what if Mrs. Kelso gave him an A? Like Papa-Ben said, it really wasn't all that great. Everyone had a heritage, even if it didn't feel like it. How did that make him special? If only he'd followed Boolkie's example and written *anything* about being Jewish!

Now a couple of police officers were inside the apartment, too. One came snooping around the kitchen. When his partner said, "Check and see if that's a note," he grabbed the paper from the counter.

"Hey!" Cobber snatched it back. "Don't read that! It's mine!"

Clara tried to pull him away, to calm him down, her hands fluttering like white birds around his head. "I'm sorry. He's upset." She rubbed his arm. "Let it be, child. They're just doing their job," she whispered in his ear.

The policeman turned sympathetic eyes on him, then moved away. *Where's Daddy?* A great buzzing numbness stole over him. His feet felt nailed to the floor. The paramedics' voices—their words—from the other side of the room sounded garbled, like static on those walkie-talkies he and Boolkie used to play with. He couldn't make sense of them. Meaning slipped away, and he couldn't watch anymore what they were doing to Papa-Ben. Why didn't his great-grandfather *move* something? A finger, his eyelids, *anything* to let Cobber see he was still okay. Still fighting. He bit his lip, trying to stop its trembling, but now he was shaking all over. Couldn't stop. Radios continued to crackle from the other room.

Please God. Please God. Please hear me and save him.

Clara slid her arm around Cobber's shoulder and made soft, shushing sounds.

"Can you see him?" he finally whispered. "Is he—"

"I don't know, sweetheart. I can't tell."

"Do you think he's going to … to make it?"

He almost missed the slight rise and fall of her shoulders. From behind her thick, clean bifocals, her gray-flannel eyes found his. "We just have to have faith … Cobber, isn't it?"

He nodded and smiled inside that she'd remembered his nickname. *Have faith.* She made it sound so easy. Was it too late to start having faith now? What if God didn't believe him? At the thought, his chin wobbled, and he reached out for Clara, a stranger he wished were Dad.

Chapter 11

After Dad arrived and took him home that night, Cobber hadn't intended to sleep. He had tried to keep his eyes open, blinking into the darkness and talking in his new way to God. Thanking Him Papa-Ben was still alive. Begging Him to keep him that way. But sometime after two, a thick, hot-tarry feeling began oozing through his limbs, pulling him down, down, down into his mattress. When the first slivers of light sliced under his window shade, he awoke with a start, sweaty and breathless, as if from a nightmare. His first thoughts were of Papa-Ben, and the bad dream turned real. Dad had promised to wake him up if there was any change. But what if he'd figured bad news could wait till morning?

I don't want to know yet. I'm not ready. Cobber pulled his blankets up beneath his chin, listening for footsteps on the stairs, bracing himself for the worst. Downstairs, the screen door slammed as Dad collected the newspaper. From the kitchen, the kettle shrilled, insistent as a buzzing alarm clock.

"Cobber? You up yet? Better get a move on!"

He peeled the blankets back reluctantly, threw on some clothes, and stalled for a while in the bathroom. Finally, he forced himself to go downstairs. "Did he … is he … okay?" he asked.

Dad looked up from the front page and set it aside. "So far, so good. He made it through the night."

"Oh, thank God." The words rushed out with his breath, surprising him. But maybe God *did* have something to do with it. "So, what do they think? Is he going to get totally better?"

"How about we go see for ourselves?"

"Right now? And miss school?"

Dad nodded. "But only a couple of classes. Grab some breakfast, okay? I have to return a call before we go."

Once Dad went off to his study, Cobber ate a bagel with cream cheese, brushed his teeth, and gathered his books. Dad's door was closed, so Cobber paced outside in the front hall. He could hear him still on the phone, but after a while, he knocked softly. "Come on, Dad," he whispered. "I'm growing a beard out here."

"Jacob, please!" His voice had a strange, hard snap to it.

Was he talking to someone from the hospital? Had Papa-Ben taken a turn for the worse? Determined to find out, he pressed his ear to the door and listened shamelessly. He had as much right as Dad did to know the truth.

"I don't understand, Mrs. Fielding," his father was saying. "His rent's paid up till the end of the month, isn't it?" He paused. "So, fine. Then how can you kick him out?"

Sounded like business—one of Dad's apartment managers having trouble with a renter. Why did business have to sneak into every little moment of their lives? More important stuff was going on.

"Let me assure you." Dad's tone had a too-patient edge. "It was an accident. Nothing to worry about."

Cobber glanced at his watch. He wished he could borrow Dad's cell phone to call Boolkie and tell him about Papa-Ben. Tell him he'd be there by second or third period, latest. But he'd seen the phone still in its charger on Dad's desk.

"I don't know what you expect *me* to do," Dad was saying.

Cobber nudged the door open and pointed to his watch. Dad held up one finger, then turned his back and lowered his voice. Cobber could only make out the words *eleven-year-old kid* and *wife*.

When Dad hung up at last, Cobber said, "So what's the problem? Somebody trip over a welcome mat and threaten to sue us again?"

"Not yet." Dad's laugh rang hollow. "You shouldn't worry about all these business things, Cobber. That's *my* job."

"Yeah, but you keep saying we're in this together."

"*Life*," Dad said, and his gaze fixed on a tiny, oval-framed picture of Mom he still kept on his desk. "Not business."

What life? he almost blurted. *All you do is work.* Instead, he eyed his shoes and thought he should tie the laces before Dad bugged him to. But he didn't. Where was that new attitude of his?

"Come on, now." Dad rumpled Cobber's hair. "Let's go see Papa-Ben. Maybe he'll feel up to talking. Heaven knows, we need to."

On the way to the hospital, Cobber tried to call Boolkie, but the answering machine picked up before any of the Bermans did. He left a brief message, saying Papa-Ben had taken too many pills and was in the hospital, that they were on their way over there to see him now.

"I'd better call school, too," Dad said.

Wouldn't want anyone thinking he'd cut class or been kidnapped on the way. Cobber nodded, pressed speed-dial, and set the phone in the hands-free cradle near his father.

By the time Dad had circled to the top of the crowded hospital parking ramp, Cobber's thoughts were racing. Would Papa-Ben be hooked up to all kinds of machines? Would he be lying there, still as death like last night, or awake but confused about where he was? *Will he even know me?* He wished Dad would tell him what to expect—how Papa-Ben would look—so he'd be ready, so he wouldn't be shocked.

In the elevator on the way down to the main floor, he studied Dad's profile: the grim set of his bearded jaw and the deep crease in his forehead. He looked like a big scared kid leading a littler scared one. Dad steered him through the hospital lobby, his hand cold on the back of Cobber's neck. When he pushed the *up* button, he avoided Cobber's eyes.

"Are you sure you told me everything?" Cobber asked at last. "What did the nurse say again?"

"That he was resting comfortably, that his condition is stable."

"What's stable mean?"

"Not changing." Dad sighed. "But he *is* going to get better. You wait and see. He's a tough old bird. Always has been."

Yeah? Then why did Dad look so grim?

When the elevator doors slapped open, they stepped in and Dad pressed 6. Someone rolled a hugely pregnant woman in a wheelchair in after them. She tried to smile at Cobber and he tried back, but neither of them was very convincing.

A strong smell of disinfectant and burnt toast blasted Cobber when they left the elevator on the sixth floor. He wrinkled his nose. Dad stopped at the nurses' desk and talked for a few moments with someone in charge. Cobber tried not to look like he was listening.

"… just for observation … holding his own … maybe tomorrow."

At the words, the knot in his throat untied itself as if by Houdini's own magic. Without waiting for Dad, he tore off down the hall, checking the names outside the patients' rooms. Esther, Gladys, Lila, Vivian. Old lady names, all of them.

"Cobber, pssst!" Dad motioned him back and pointed to the corridor beyond the nurses' station. "This way. I guess he was asking for you."

"For me? Really?" He wondered whether to be happy about that—or nervous.

Ben Kuper, Bed Two was written in red ink on a wall sticker outside room 625. The door was open. Soft snoring came from the curtained area near the window. Cobber tugged at Dad's sleeve. "If he's sleeping," he whispered, "maybe we should come back later."

But Dad ignored him, continued past an empty bed, and drew the curtain aside. Cobber's breath caught at the sight of his great-grandfather, so tiny and pale in the huge white bed. He tiptoed closer. Papa-Ben's hair was uncombed—like it had been the night before—and his mouth sagged open just enough for Cobber to see that some of his false teeth were missing. He'd hate them seeing him like that. Cobber wondered where those dentures were.

A monitor beeped out a steady beat. One clear plastic line drained into Papa-Ben's arm from a bag suspended over the bed. Cobber inched closer and eased the soft, silvery-gray tufts back down with his hand. Papa-Ben's eyelids fluttered. His lips moved soundlessly. Cobber held his breath, wondering what his great-grandfather might say.

"Papa," Dad said gently, crossing to the other side of the bed, "it's Larry. And Jacob's here, too."

"Yacobe?" The name sounded like a prayer, the way he said it. "My Yacobe?"

"Yeah, it's me." Cobber took Papa-Ben's cold hand and tried to warm it between both of his own.

Papa-Ben's eyelids seemed to struggle for a moment, then lifted. His eyes, the same watery blue of a swimming pool, stared blankly at Cobber. But after a few seconds, he blinked and a smile warmed his face. "Ah, Yacobe, you *are* here. Thank God."

"Thank God about *you*," Cobber blurted. "I … I prayed for you, Papa-Ben. And … and it worked."

"Good boy. You see?"

Cobber hung his head. All this God stuff, his talk about praying, felt too new—and almost awkward. Like trying to speak with a mouthful of marbles. "So, how do you feel?"

"Alive, eh? But why am I in this place?"

Cobber looked to Dad, unsure what to say.

"It seems you got your pills mixed up yesterday," Dad said, "that you took too many. Do you remember any of that?"

Papa-Ben frowned. "Not really."

Cobber remembered all too well—the empty plastic boxes and pill bottles, and the policeman looking at Jacob's haiku. "Whatever happened, Papa-Ben," he said, "I'm glad you're okay now."

Dad leaned in closer. His hand smoothed the pillow case above Papa-Ben's head. "You're usually so careful, Papa. I don't understand."

"What is to understand?" Papa-Ben slipped his hand out and laid it on Cobber's. "I made a mistake. I called Yacobe."

Cobber frowned. Did he mean he made a mistake, taking the pills, or a mistake, wasting time calling *him* instead of 911? Dad must have been wondering the same thing. He looked at Papa-Ben, his eyes dark with questions. Cobber tried his voice, but it wouldn't work.

"What was a mistake, Papa?" Dad asked, finally.

"The pills!" Papa-Ben raised his voice. "I got confused. I could not remember if I had taken them."

"It's okay, Papa. I didn't mean to upset you." Dad breathed again, and Cobber did, too. He'd done his best to get help right away. "The main thing now is to get you on your feet."

Papa-Ben nodded. "I do not like it here. The service, you know. It is something awful."

Dad grinned. "Sounds like tomorrow can't come soon enough, huh?"

"Tomorrow?" Papa-Ben raised one bushy eyebrow. "This is what they are saying? I can go home tomorrow?"

"Yes," Cobber broke in, "isn't that great? It'll be Saturday, right? So I can spend all day over there and—"

"Cobber," Dad cut in. He patted the air the way he did when he wanted Cobber to get out of his office and let him talk in private.

But Cobber pressed his lips together and clamped his hands around the side rail on Papa-Ben's bed. No way he was going anywhere.

Dad heaved a great sigh but didn't force the issue. "Mrs. Fielding called me this morning bright and early," he said to Papa-Ben. "She's ... concerned."

"Mrs. Fielding?" Papa-Ben's voice, Cobber's question.

"You know. The administrator lady over at the center."

Papa-Ben nodded, and Dad pressed on. "You've ... we've got a problem, Papa. She says you can't—they won't let you—go home." Papa-Ben just blinked. "Do you understand what I'm saying?"

"Sure. But—"

"That's not fair!" Cobber's cheeks went hot. "She can't do that, can she?"

"How can this be, Larry? Where will I go?"

"Dad, *do* something! Call your lawyer!"

Dad shrugged helplessly, and Cobber hated seeing all the fight knocked out of him before they'd even begun. "There's a policy. She says she's sorry, it's nothing personal. They all love you over there, you know that. They just feel you need a level of care now that they can't provide."

"A level of care? Speak English, Larry."

"They're concerned about your accident, Papa. Your ... forgetfulness."

Cobber avoided Papa-Ben's eyes. He swallowed hard. *It's my fault you're here!* If only he'd broken his promise and told Dad about the eggs and the flood and all the other stuff! His father could have taken charge, gotten some kind of help. Then none of this would have happened. He wondered now whether some promises were better off broken.

"Unfortunately, there are no beds available in the nursing home wing," Dad went on. "And, legally, their hands are tied. They don't want to be responsible."

"Nobody *asked* them to," Cobber said.

Papa-Ben patted his hand, trying to calm him. "So, what is an old man to do, eh? Nobody wants to be responsible anymore."

Responsible. The word echoed in Cobber's mind. He remembered how the rabbi had commented on his having a lot of responsibility. But he could feel the rightness of it now—that it wasn't something to run from. Look at Dad. He'd never run from responsibility in his life. Cobber turned to his father. "*We'll* be responsible, won't we, Dad?" Maybe *this* is what Mom's Ouija board message meant: *Be a family.* A *real* family, all living together. "Move in with us, Papa-Ben," he said. "We've got plenty of room."

Chapter 12

The cafeteria's din surrounded Cobber as he and Boolkie scooted to the far end of a table near the door. He watched Boolkie lay out his two cartons of milk, double fries, and fruit roll. No doubt Mrs. Berman would have an attack if she knew what his idea of a good lunch was. Not that Cobber's slab of greasy pizza and red juice box were much better. But then he didn't have a mother to report to at the end of the day—the only bright side he could see to *that* situation. Finally, he caught Boolkie up on what had happened at the hospital.

"I bet Dad's mad I put him on the spot like that, wanting Papa-Ben to live with us," he said.

"I wouldn't worry, if I were you. He'll probably get busy and forget to be annoyed."

"Yeah, probably." Cobber nibbled at his pizza crust. It tasted like cardboard. "How can they just kick Papa-Ben out like that?"

"Maybe it's for his own good." Boolkie shrugged. "Who knows?"

"*I* know, that's who. He's not some crazy old man they can throw away like garbage."

Boolkie twitched his lips to one side but said nothing.

"What?"

"Never mind."

"You think he *is* crazy, don't you?"

"Not crazy. But maybe just … losing it?"

Cobber peeled the wrapper from his straw, stabbed it into the juice box, and sighed. "The truth is, he *is* getting kind of forgetful. I knew that, but he made me promise not to tell Dad. And …" He debated whether to say more. "And a promise is a promise."

Boolkie looked down at his French fries. He picked out the longest ones and laid them on his tray side by side, neatening the edges the way Cobber did his pencils. "Sometimes promises have to be broken," he said finally. "And *some*times people should understand that."

"So you're saying this is all *my* fault?"

"No, I'm not." Boolkie clicked his tongue, and Cobber realized Boolkie must have been talking about his own broken promise. "Man, you're the one who saved him."

"Yeah, once I realized it was *him* and not you, messing around. Don't do that anymore—imitate his accent—okay?"

"At your request, sir, I shall remove it from my repertoire." Boolkie pretended to open a notebook and cross something off the page. "Anything else?"

Cobber rolled his eyes. "Not that I can think of, but I'll let you know."

"I am sure that you vill," Boolkie said in his best Count Dracula voice.

Better the Count than Papa-Ben. Cobber fell silent and thought again about his great-grandfather. Where *was* he going to live? Dad had made light of the idea of having him move in with them, and Papa-Ben himself had insisted he didn't want to be a bother. Still, Papa-Ben hated nursing homes, and the one at the center was full, anyway. What was left?

"Hey, Cobber, you want to come over today? Maybe work on your act? You haven't changed your mind, have you?"

"What? No Hebrew?"

"Naw. It's Sabbath, my day of rest." Boolkie grinned.

"What does that mean, anyway?"

"Ex-squeeze me?"

"Sabbath. You wrote your haiku about it, like you guys are such perfect Jews. And I'm just wondering, you know, because your dad works on Saturdays and your mom drives you places and you go to the mall sometimes and spend money and, well, I'm just saying, that's not *really* the way you're supposed to keep the Sabbath, right?" Cobber felt suddenly dizzy. What was he doing, trying to pick a fight with Boolkie?

"What's with you, man? Chill. I was just making a joke."

"I know. You're always making jokes. But I was *trying* to be serious."

"About Sabbath? Jeez, what's up with that?"

"You and your stupid Hebrew," Cobber said. "It's got me

thinking, that's all. And what I don't get is why *you* feel so Jewish and I *don't*."

"Who says I feel *any*thing? I just do what my parents want me to do."

"Yeah, but why don't *they* follow all the rules, then?"

"Hello? Earth to Cobber. Have you noticed where we live? Maybe in New York Dad could close on Saturdays and not lose a ton of money, but you think we can do that here? Especially when the tourists are gone? Jeez, that's our busiest day."

Cobber considered what it must have been like for Papa-Ben, moving from the big city where there were lots of Jewish people to this little town where there were hardly any.

"I hear they even close schools there for the High Holy Days," Boolkie said. "That'd never happen here, that's for sure."

"You can say that again." Cobber tried to imagine not having to choose between going to school and going to temple on those important days. Why should any kid *have* to? They didn't make all the Christians decide whether to go to school on Christmas, did they? "I can't even imagine it."

"Yeah, well, who cares if we're not perfect?" Boolkie said. "It's not like you can flunk being Jewish in America, you know."

Cobber pictured Rabbi Brahms standing at the temple's front door, telling people they couldn't come in because they'd messed up Sabbath and weren't good enough Jews. Not a chance he'd ever do that. And even Dad had said being Jewish was all about making choices.

"So, you wanna come over today or not? Polish up your act?"

Like I'm really going to go through with this. But all he said was, "Sounds good. You can help me decide which tricks to do."

"Yeah, for sure." Boolkie started dunking his fries in ketchup double-time. "When's Papa-Ben getting out of the hospital, anyway?"

"Tomorrow, supposedly. I almost wish they'd keep him longer. Give us some time … you know … to figure something out."

"Maybe your dad will say yes, and he can move in with you guys."

"I don't know, Boolk. The more I think about it, the more impossible it seems. I mean, what about the stairs? And who's going to watch him all day when I'm at school?"

Boolkie didn't answer. He kept tapping his fingers on the edge of the table, zoning out totally.

"Hello? Earth to Boolkie." Cobber rapped his knuckles to get his friend's attention.

Boolkie blinked, then smiled, and Cobber could see the wheels turning behind the glint in his eyes.

"What are *you* grinning about?" Cobber asked.

Boolkie raised his eyebrows a couple of times. "Why doesn't your dad work at *your* house? I mean, he has an office there, anyway, right?"

"Hey, yeah! And I could go straight home after school." Cobber didn't realize he'd been squeezing his drink box until juice squirted out. He mopped it up with his napkin. "And I suppose I *could* survive not walking you to temple."

"A small sacrifice, I'd say."

"Yeah, miniscule." Cobber stared at his pizza, trying to picture Papa-Ben living with them. What about trying out for basketball next season? Was Cobber ready to ditch that team, too, along with soccer? At least Coach let him play. What about movies at the mall and frisbee-golf at the park? As much as he loved Papa-Ben, would his living there mean Cobber would have to give up being a kid? Once more the rabbi's words—*a lot of responsibility*—echoed through his mind, and this time he wasn't so sure whether that was a good thing or not.

"Hey, snap out of it!"

When Cobber looked up, Boolkie had French fries hanging out of his nose and ears. Cobber fired off a squirt of juice at him, but missed.

"Jeez, Cobber, I thought you'd never notice." Boolkie laughed and shook the fries loose. "So? Do you still think it's so impossible, having Papa-Ben move in? You think you can convince your dad?"

Cobber shrugged. "No offense, Boolk," he said, "but there's somebody else I want to talk to first."

* * * *

Cobber took the bus home to collect his magic act supplies, then biked to Boolkie's. From the moment he stepped into Mrs. Berman's kitchen, alive with the rich aroma of baking challah, he knew he'd come to the right place. Even if he didn't get the advice he needed, he'd get a dose of Mom-feeling, and that could only help. Now the sweet root-beer smell of something she was scooping from a squat blue-lidded jar snaked through the room. No wonder he and Dad never celebrated Sabbath. He couldn't imagine either one of them making all the same preparations as Mrs. Berman. It was a lot of work to go through for only two people.

When she saw him, Mrs. Berman stopped grating carrots and went down to the deli to get the boys' favorite after-school snacks—strawberry blintzes for Cobber and peanut-butter-on-a-boolkie for Guess Who.

"There you go, boys. Enjoy." She set the plates before them and lingered for a long, awkward moment, fussing with the arrangement of the paper napkin holder, the salt, the pepper. Cobber recognized the gesture. At last, she took her hand away and let her fingers play with her short blonde curls. "Cobber?" When he looked up, she offered only an apologetic shrug. "I've missed you around here. That's all."

"Well, I've missed being here." He glanced sideways at Boolkie, tossing him the blame.

"Are you … okay?" she asked.

"Me? Yeah. I'm fine," he lied.

She looked at him then, and Cobber knew by the way her eyes flicked away that she saw right through him.

He cleared his throat—and the awkward silence between

them. "You know about Papa-Ben, don't you." A statement, not a question.

She nodded. "I talked to your dad, after we got your message."

"After we'd gone to the hospital?" And after I opened my big mouth about Papa-Ben living with us?

Again, she nodded. "Boolkie, do me a favor, honey, will you? Go tell Eli I want to see that rough draft of his speech before dinner, okay?"

"Think I can't take a hint?" Boolkie rose abruptly, picking up his plate. "If you want to get rid of me, Ma, all you have to do is ask."

"Honey, that's not what I—"

"It's okay. Really. We went all through this at lunch." He turned to Cobber. "When you're ready to hang up your worry-wart badge and kick back a little, you know where to find me."

Mrs. Berman shot him a look. "Please. He's got a lot on his mind."

"Yeah, well …" His voice trailed off. "If he wants to get a lot *off* his mind, he'll hang with *me*." He turned to Cobber. "Let me know when you wanna practice."

"Thanks." Heat flooded Cobber's cheeks. Boolkie was right. Cobber loved how chill he felt whenever they were together. Left to his own devices, he might chew on his worries forever.

After Boolkie had gone, Cobber eyed his blintzes. Mrs. Berman had topped them with extra powdered sugar and butter, just the way he liked. Strangely, though, he had no desire to eat. "So, what did Dad say? Where's Papa-Ben going to live?"

Mrs. Berman took the chair beside him. She pressed her lips together before answering. "All day—while you've been at school—he's ... he's been looking into nursing homes, Cobber." He winced at the words. "You may have to go all the way to Janesville or Racine to find a bed."

Find a bed, find a bed. The words raced through his mind, and he pictured Dad prowling the junk yard and garage sales, looking for a bed. As if Papa-Ben didn't already have one of his own. "No way! That's like, at least an hour from here. By car!"

"I know. Believe me, he's not happy about it either."

"But why *can't* he live with us?" Cobber blurted. Now his eyes were hot, too, and he blinked quickly. "What's that saying? Where there's a will, there's a way? You know what *I* think?"

"No. What?"

"Dad just doesn't want to be bothered. He doesn't want to have to worry about anything besides work."

"Cobber." Mrs. Berman clicked her tongue. "You don't think he worries about *you*?"

Cobber shrugged. "I guess he does. He tries. But shoot, Papa-Ben's his *grand*father! He can't just ship him off somewhere and let strangers worry about him. If *he* won't, why should they?"

"I know you don't want to hear this, but finding

professional care for Papa-Ben at this point does make some sense. Your dad is just not equipped to work *and* take care of him. There's only so much one person can do in a day."

Those juggled people-balls bounced through his mind. "So, you think we *should* send him away?" His voice rose and, since she'd already arranged all the condiments, he clenched his hands into fists beneath the table. This was *not* what he had come to hear. She was supposed to be on *his* side. On Papa-Ben's. Not on Dad's.

"I didn't say that." Mrs. Berman sighed. "Oh, honey, I wish your mother were here, for more reasons than one." She rubbed her nose. Cobber had never before noticed how red it could get. "God, I miss her, and I was only her friend, not her child."

At her words, Cobber's own nose started itching like crazy. But he would not cry. Not here. Not now. He steadied himself with a great breath and carefully let it go. "What would she do," he asked at last, "if she *were* here?"

"Well, there'd be no question. Papa-Ben would live at your house. And if she couldn't watch him herself, she'd hire home health aides, get Meals on Wheels—I volunteer there, you know. Whatever it took, there'd be no question. Beth would *make* it work."

"Papa-Ben says I'm a lot like her." Cobber's voice was so soft, he could barely hear it.

"You are. It's true. You both have a big heart for people."

Had. Mom *had,* past tense. It wasn't the first time he'd noticed Mrs. Berman talking about her as if she were still alive. He wondered why that was, why he couldn't feel that way, too.

"If that's what *she'd* do," he said and nodded firmly, "then that's what I'll do."

Boolkie must have cranked up the volume on some computer game, because suddenly it blared, filling the flat, shaking the walls. Mrs. Berman patted his hand, maybe figuring she'd said enough, that she should let him go hang with Boolkie. Still, he didn't move.

"Will you please help me, Mrs. B? Convince Dad, first of all, and then find out what else we need?"

"Of course, I will, honey. But I think you've got it backwards." When he frowned, she went on. "First, we get our ducks in line, and *then* we talk to your father," she said. "I've known him a long time, long enough to know that our actions will speak much louder than our ideas."

"I-I guess you're right." Cobber looked at those blintzes. They were finally whispering to him. He picked up his fork, then stopped. "Do you really think we can pull it off in a day?"

"What was that you said, Cobber?" Mrs. Berman ruffled his hair and the feel of her hand set his eyes itching again. "Where there's a will, there's a way?"

He matched her smile with his own and felt the last shred of worry slip away. All at once, he was ravenous.

* * * *

Cobber nudged Boolkie's door open with the toe of his sneaker. Piles of laundry provided resistance, and he had to yell over the computer volume. "Hey, Boolk! You ready?"

Boolkie turned with a start, then clicked off the video. Cobber dropped his backpack on the unmade bed.

"Let's see what you brought." Boolkie flopped on his bed. "It's so awesome you're going to do this!"

"Yeah, well, I'm not so sure. You'd tell me if I suck, wouldn't you?"

"I would. Believe me. I don't want a repeat of third grade any more than you do."

"Don't remind me." Cobber sighed, and fumbled around in his backpack. At last, he pulled out an unsharpened pencil, a piece of plain paper, a pair of scissors, an empty plastic soda bottle, two blue paper plates, and some wrapped Starburst candies. "I need a ketchup packet," he said. "Think you could snag one from the deli?"

"Sure. Be right back."

While Boolkie was gone, Cobber cleared a space on the desk and hurried to set up his tricks. He didn't want Boolkie to see how they were done. It would spoil everything. A tickle of excitement shot through him at the thought of fooling his friend. But wasn't he also fooling Boolkie by pretending he was actually going to perform at the talent show? A liar *and* a promise breaker. That was a new combination.

Cobber shook his head. He tried to imagine actually going through with it—the Great Cobberini, the announcer might say. It sounded better than Yacoberto. He'd stride to the center of the stage as if he'd never even heard of stage fright. As if that awful oral report episode had never happened. As if nobody remembered or even thought about it anymore. He'd look out at the audience—all those eyes staring right through him—and … Cobber blew out a quick breath, ripping himself from the scene. Boolkie could believe what he wanted, but there was no way Cobber was actually going to do this.

Boolkie returned with a few ketchup packets then, and Cobber filled the plastic bottle with water, pushing one packet through the opening.

"Okay, so pretend this is it. The big night. What's your setup? What are you going to say?" Boolkie asked.

"I guess I'd need a little stand. Maybe a table cloth."

"What will you wear? I mean, you have to look the part, you know?"

"I don't know. I haven't thought about it." And I won't, either. Because this isn't happening.

Boolkie cleared off his nightstand and dragged it between the bed and Cobber. "Okay. Do your thing. Pretend I'm the audience."

Cobber blew out a long breath. "Ladies and gentlemen, boys and girls, I have a piece of paper." He showed the back and the front. "Nothing special. Just a regular piece of paper. Does anyone think I can cut a hole big enough to walk through?"

Boolkie clapped his hands and hooted. "Naw, I don't think so. Prove it."

"I will do just that." Cobber folded the paper in half and proceeded to cut it this way and that, until finally a huge circle of paper emerged that he could actually step through.

Boolkie looked impressed. "Good one. You should keep that. It's a big trick. Everyone can see it. Not like card tricks."

Cobber considered his repertoire. "So no Jumping Jacks?"

Boolkie shook his head. For his next trick Cobber made the packet of ketchup rise and fall mysteriously inside the plastic bottle. "More distraction with your right hand," Boolkie said. "Snap your fingers or something."

Cobber made a mental note.

"And stand up straight like you're confident."

"But I'm not."

"I know. But you can fake it till you make it, can't you?"

"I-I guess." As he proceeded through his other tricks— the disappearing candies, the magnetic pencil—he realized he was actually enjoying himself. But maybe it wasn't the magic itself or the idea of the show. Maybe it was just about hanging out with Boolkie again.

"You gotta keep talking," Boolkie said when Cobber had finished. "Keep them wanting more, you know?"

"How about you do the talking and I do the tricks?" Cobber suggested. "If I don't have to open my mouth, maybe I won't throw up."

"Fun-ny. You're such a kidder."

Ha, Cobber thought. If only Boolkie knew the truth.

Chapter 13

When Mrs. Berman dropped Cobber and his bike off at home, to his surprise, Dad's big chef knife was chattering away in the kitchen. He'd almost gotten used to having McDonald's, Taco Bell, or pizza every night. Maybe his father was feeling guilty and fixing stir-fry—the only way Cobber would eat lots of vegetables. Whoever thought a kid could get sick of fast food? Even eating *green* food sounded better. Mom would be proud.

He squeezed his eyes shut extra tight at the thought. Good. He could still bring back his own little movie of her trying to get him to eat green beans, broccoli, spinach, and some weird-looking thing with spiny green-and-purplish leaves. And he could still see those cheese, butter, and "cauliflower mashed potato" disguises she'd tried on him, too. But Mom's face was getting blurry. The center looked all rainbowy, like a drop of oil in a puddle. Was he starting to forget her? Cobber swallowed hard. He'd eat all those green things at once if only that would bring her back.

His attention snapped back to the stir-fry. While Dad's cooking was simple—nothing like the Sabbath dinner Mrs. Berman was rushing home to serve—at least he was there and not out buying fast food again.

"Hi, Dad!" Cobber called from the mudroom, tossing his jacket on the washing machine, then hurrying down the hall. He wondered whether his father had more news from the hospital. What if something had happened to Papa-Ben? Though Cobber tried not to think the worst, it was like telling himself not to think about elephants. That only made a herd of them lumber around his brain. He realized he'd been so worried all day about where Papa-Ben would live, that he had just assumed he'd be all right. Now, all the what-ifs made his pulse race. He burst into the kitchen, suddenly breathless with worry. "He's still okay, isn't he?"

"Papa-Ben? Of course he is." Dad set his knife down, placing his hands squarely on Cobber's shoulders. His fingers reeked of garlic. Cobber felt their strength and warmth through his shirt. "That grandpa of ours is going to see one hundred easy."

Easy? Seven months could be a really long time, considering the way the past week had gone. "Are we going to see him tonight?" he asked.

"Maybe. But first we've got to talk." Dad swept a bunch of mushrooms and onions into the frying pan with the blade of his knife but didn't light the burner. He turned to Cobber again, and though his face smiled, his eyes were those of that same scared big kid from the hospital. Cobber braced himself for something worse than the scolding he'd been expecting. He really hadn't meant to put Dad on the spot. "I, um, I've been thinking about Papa-Ben's situation," Dad said, "about where he could go."

Cobber held his breath, waiting for no, he can't live here and yes, he's going to a nursing home.

"It's a big decision. I wish Gail and Bob lived closer."

Cobber nodded. Dad's younger sister and brother lived about as far from Wisconsin as they could get, and in opposite directions, one on each coast. "Did you at least call them? What did they say?"

"Same thing they always say when I ask their advice. 'It's not your responsibility, Larry. Find a good place for Papa-Ben and take care of Jacob. Let us know what we can do.'"

"Yeah, right." Cobber hadn't meant for the words to slip out. But from what he could tell, they were the checkbook kind of relatives, both of them. He wondered what they would do if Papa-Ben *did* live near them. Probably nothing different.

"Yeah, right? What's *that* supposed to mean? They do their share."

"If you say so." Cobber shrugged, picked a slice of raw mushroom from the pan, and popped it into his mouth. "So, what *are* we going to do?"

"*We* are not going to do anything."

"What? We have to—"

"You're the kid, I'm the dad. *I* take care of business, remember?"

"But this isn't business. It's family."

"Oh, Cobber." Dad shook his head. "You sound just like your mother."

"I thought that was a good thing."

"It's a *frustrating* thing." Dad tugged at the gray tuft in his neatly trimmed beard. "*I* see how many hours there are in a day, how much of me there is to spread around. How little, actually." He made a soft *tsk*ing sound. "But not your mother. Somehow God blessed her with thirty-hour days and she packed them to the gills, every last one. I don't know how she did it."

Cobber cringed at Dad's talk of God *blessing* Mom. Maybe it was just an expression—something people said— but hearing those two words together made him squirm. It was God, after all, who had given her an exploding balloon-thing in her brain—an *aneurysm*, they called it. Some blessing *that* was! Dad was a fine one to talk about God at all. He hardly ever set foot in the temple anymore, and he acted like it was a real pain, getting up early every week to take Cobber to Sunday school.

Still, hadn't God answered Cobber's prayer and saved Papa-Ben?

"Why are you looking at me that way?" Dad asked. "It's true. She always made time for everybody, and you do, too. To be honest"—Dad avoided Cobber's eyes—"you put me to shame, visiting Papa-Ben as often as you do."

"But you could fix all that, don't you see? We *both* could." New hope bubbled up inside him. He knew the plan was for Mrs. Berman to talk to Dad, but he couldn't let this moment, this *opportunity*, go. "Bring him here. Let him live with us."

Dad rubbed his beard for a long moment, then shook his head. "It wouldn't work. Maybe if your mom were here …" He glanced about the kitchen, as if trying to convince himself she wasn't.

But Cobber knew better. Besides the framed wildflowers, there were reminders everywhere. Mom's handwritten recipes, neatly collected in a binder. Blue-glazed pottery canisters she'd made in a college ceramics class. Even a little basket of dried rose petals she had saved sat on the counter near the stove. "I'm telling you, Dad, we could do it! It would be so cool, like a real family again. I'd have someone to come home to, and at night, we could all sit around the table and talk during dinner." He could picture it so clearly, like a movie playing behind his eyes. That Ouija board message was starting to make sense.

"That's not how it would be." Dad's sigh seemed to fill the whole room.

"But it *could* be, don't you see? You could work at home—you do that a lot anyway—and I could come straight here on the bus. And when I'm at school, we could have those Meals on Wheels people come. Mrs. Berman volunteers there and—"

"Whoa. Hold on, Cobber. There are all kinds of things you're not considering."

"Like?"

"Like, he's a hundred years old, practically, and needs professional medical care. Like, your need to be a kid. Like, my crazy work hours. Like …" He said nothing for an agonizingly long time. Finally, he lit the burner and turned back again. Clunking ice cubes shattered the silence.

Cobber could almost see Dad's words knotted up in his throat behind his Adam's apple. He wanted to shake them loose. "Just *say* it!"

"I want to protect you, okay? Is that so wrong?" Dad turned away again to attend to the stir-fry. His pinstriped shirt seemed to wall Cobber out.

"Protect me from *what*? Jeez, I'm not five years old anymore. I'm not a baby."

Dad's shoulders rose and fell. The oil began to hiss in the pan. Finally, Cobber tugged at his arm.

When Dad turned toward him again, his eyes were rimmed with red. "A little boy shouldn't have to watch everyone he loves die."

Papa-Ben had said almost the same thing about burying his wife and children. But Cobber had lost only Mom, so far. Not everyone. At the thought, he knocked on a wooden cabinet so as not to jinx himself. Dad, on the other hand, had buried his wife and *both* parents. Losing Papa-Ben would hit him hard. *Oh, Dad,* he wanted to say, *who are you really trying to protect? Yourself or me?* Something melted inside him then, and he wished he could hug Dad, wished Dad would hug him back. But his father had already returned to stirring the vegetables.

"Dad," he said finally, "an old man shouldn't have to live—to *die*—with strangers. Listen to me. I know we can make it work."

"Cobber, what if he gets sick? Has a stroke? Can't get around? Are you prepared to lift him, wash him, clean him up? I've got to tell you, *I'm* not. That's why we've got to find a nursing home for him."

The words *nursing* and *home* refused to make sense. Still, Cobber winced, imagining Papa-Ben as Dad had just described him. It was almost impossible to picture, though, because as old as Papa-Ben was, he didn't look or act his age. Dad was right about one thing, though. At nearly one hundred, *anything* could happen to Papa-Ben. At any time. Cobber had to make every moment count. All at once, something else hit him. And age had nothing to do with it. Mom was proof of that. The truth was, anything could happen to *anyone*. To Dad. Or to himself, even. Then what would Dad do? Send *him* away?

"See?" Dad said. "I thought so. Not a pretty picture, is it?"

Cobber gaped at his father. He couldn't wrap his mind around his father's words. Dad assumed he *agreed* with him! Fire burned in his cheeks. "I can't believe you, Dad. Babies come with dirty diapers, don't they? Does that mean you shouldn't love them and take care of them? What if *you* got sick? What if *I* did, huh? *Then* what would you do? Get rid of me?"

Without waiting for a reply, he stormed from the kitchen, filled up with the rightness of his anger. He felt bigger, older, smarter. Surely Dad would see that, would listen to him. Flopping on his bed, he stared up at the ceiling. Something gnawed at his insides, and it wasn't only hunger. He wished he could find those friendly plaster-swirl animal faces that used to get him through naptime when he was a kid. But those had gone away when Mom did.

Maybe Mrs. Berman would call and talk to Dad, but he doubted it. How could she have had time to put anything together for Papa-Ben? She was busy getting Sabbath dinner on the table and rushing everyone off to temple. Eli was required to go, and now Boolkie probably was, too. Cobber wondered whether they'd all keep going, once their bar mitzvahs were over, or whether high school football games and concerts and plays would win out over temple on Friday nights. He supposed all over America Jews had to make the same choice every week. Why couldn't their Sabbath be on Sunday like everyone else's?

His haiku echoed in his mind: Me? I am nothing. No culture, no heritage.

No heritage. As if he'd already made a choice *not* to be Jewish. But he really hadn't, had he? No wonder Papa-Ben had been upset.

Cobber's stomach growled. But there was no way he was going to go downstairs and apologize to Dad. If he waited long enough, surely Dad would come up here. Slapping in a rap CD, he cranked the volume up. High. High enough to make the walls dance. Then he put away his piles of clean laundry and tidied up stacks of magazines that had collapsed all over the floor. At last he pulled out a scarf and worked on his Magic Appearing Act in front of the full-length mirror on a sliding panel of his closet.

When Dad finally banged on his door, Cobber bit back a grin, pocketed the scarf, turned the music down, and let him in.

"That's *one* way to make me come to my senses." Dad gave an exaggerated shudder.

Cobber said nothing. Was it only the music that had brought him upstairs?

Dad stuffed his hands in his pockets and hunched his shoulders. "I-I'm sorry, Cobber. What you said down there … it really made me think. Can't say I like the way you said it, but, hey." He gave only a twitch of a smile. "So, how much humble pie are you gonna make me eat, huh?"

"Humble pie? Is that like shepherd's pie? I thought we were having chicken." Cobber held his breath, not wanting to say too much. It wasn't often that Dad admitted he'd been wrong. Why spoil their truce by pressing the issue about Papa-Ben? Maybe he should leave it to Mrs. Berman, the way they'd planned.

"Go on," Dad said. "Out with it, mister."

Cobber hesitated.

"Seriously. Tell me."

"I don't know, but … well, I was just thinking, and—"

"Cobber!"

"Don't you think it's how Papa-Ben is *today* that counts. I mean—"

"Who are *we* to predict the future?" Dad asked.

Cobber nodded.

"Yes, son. Absolutely. What's important *is* today."

They stared at each other for a long, awkward moment. At last Dad broke the silence. "So"—he clapped Cobber on the shoulder, not quite a hug, but Cobber warmed to his touch—"guess we'd better start making plans for Papa-Ben's homecoming, huh?"

"Here? You mean it?" His voice came out in a squeak.

"There's a home care agency over by my office. Devoted Guardians, I think. Let me call them."

"Really? All right!" Cobber high-fived his father. "So when are we bringing him home?"

Home. He turned the word over silently as if he were saying it, feeling it for the first time. Not just 741 Sheridan Lane, but a new and better place, somewhere he really wanted to be.

Chapter 14

Dad let Cobber listen in on the extension when he told Papa-Ben their decision. "We're going to pack up your place tomorrow and get you moved—all right?—so we can't come by to pick you up," he explained. "Not till late."

"Take your time, Larry. Now they are wanting me to stay until Sunday."

"Really? Is there a problem?" Dad asked the question before Cobber could.

Cobber held his breath.

"No, I am fine. Do not worry. They just want to watch and be sure."

"Well, okay then. That'll give us a little more time to get your room ready."

"You are sure they can do this?" Papa-Ben asked. "Make me leave my own home?"

"Unfortunately, yes."

Cobber wriggled in the awkward silence. Finally, Papa-Ben cleared his throat. "Bless you, Larry. At least you tried. And I promise, I will be like a mouse. You will not even know I am there, eh? You got mending? I will do it, no charge. Just don't tell my union." Papa-Ben's laugh turned quickly into a cough, then at last, faded away.

"You behave yourself now, hear?" Dad said. "Don't give those nurses a hard time."

"Who, me?"

Cobber could imagine the teasing look on Papa-Ben's face. No doubt they all argued over who got to take care of him—and he knew it.

After they hung up, Cobber raced to Dad's study. "Where *is* his room going to be?" he asked. Surely Dad didn't expect Papa-Ben to climb stairs to the extra bedroom, and it wasn't likely he'd give up his study. Not in a day, anyway. It would take a month of shoveling to clear out all the papers, not to mention the piles of newspapers, books, and magazines. Besides, where would Dad work then? That left only the living-and-dining room, the kitchen, and the family room on the main floor. That, and a little bathroom. "Houston," Cobber said, "I think we have a problem."

Dad shrugged. "The way I see it, we either give him the family room or the living room. All they do is collect dust, anyway. Take your pick."

Cobber considered his choices. He and Boolkie usually hung out in the family room, watching TV or videos. The living room, on the other hand, still held all Mom's treasures—miniature crystal figurines and her Grandmother Cohen's antique perfume bottles. If Mom's spirit hung out anywhere in the house, it would be in that room. A *living* room. It almost seemed sacred.

"Let's give him the family room," Cobber said, finally. "It's more private back there and … well, it's for family, isn't it?"

"Yes, it is." Dad chucked him gently beneath the chin. "Now why don't you go get some of your reading done, while I call the agency? Tomorrow will be here before we know it."

* * * *

The next morning while Dad was off renting a truck with a guy from his office, Cobber called Boolkie to see if he wanted to help. Since the deli was always packed on Saturdays, Boolkie was glad for a good excuse to get out of there before he got "volunteered" to work. Once Dad drove them to Papa-Ben's, their job was to put things in boxes, while Dad and his friend hauled the heavy stuff.

Now Cobber hesitated in the apartment doorway, feeling suddenly uneasy. The lemony smell from Papa-Ben's neighbor lady and his aftershave still hung in the air, and the horror of seeing him laid out on the floor came flooding back. The sooner they got in and out of there, the better.

"Must have been creepy, being here, seeing him," Boolkie said.

"Yeah. Even creepier than you reading my mind."

"Not your mind, man. Your face. You look like you're gonna lose your breakfast."

Cobber swallowed the spit that was pooling under his tongue and forced himself into the narrow kitchen. Papa-Ben's empty plastic pill container was still on the counter. He swept it into a box before he had time to think about it.

Then they started on the cupboards, wrapping Papa-Ben's few chipped dishes in newspaper. Cobber had never noticed before how bare the place was. Not that Papa-Ben had to cook much. The center served lunch and dinner downstairs in the dining room. And how hard was it to pour a bowl of Corn Flakes—or boil an egg? Cobber wished he hadn't thought about that again.

"Hey, guys," Dad said, "don't forget to label those boxes."

Boolkie rolled his eyes. "Yeah, right. Like he's ever going to need these things."

"Don't argue," Cobber said. "It's easier to just do what he says."

In the drawers, they found an assortment of mismatched silverware, potholders, rubber bands, coiled twine, and bread knives. One in particular caught Cobber's eye. The handle was decorated with Hebrew letters made of bits of turquoise. "What's this say?" he asked.

Boolkie looked closer, then shrugged. "What do you expect? I've only had a few classes."

Cobber picked it up as if it were some holy object and gazed at the sharp, scalloped blade. Over the years, how many Sabbath challahs had this knife cut? Did Papa-Ben keep using it once his daughter—Cobber's grandma Rachel Stern—and all the others had died? A sudden shiver worked its way up his spine. He set the knife down abruptly, as if he'd just been zapped by an electric charge.

"Hey, whatsa matter wit choo?" Boolkie turned on his Italian accent.

"I-I don't know. Is it cold in here?"

Boolkie shrugged.

"Sorry, Boolk, but I've got to get out of here. You'll finish up?"

"Sure."

"Good. I'll go start in the bedroom, okay?"

Dad and his friend had already carted off Papa-Ben's recliner and coffee table, leaving the living room practically bare. Cobber stared at the four little squares imprinted in the carpet, marking the place where Papa-Ben usually sat. The apartment had no center now. Everything felt off balance. Including him.

He reeled into the bedroom, then sat on Papa-Ben's bed—it was narrow and covered by another scratchy rainbow-colored afghan. One more reminder of Great-Grandma Dvosha, one Papa-Ben could wrap himself in, like her arms. Cobber's pulse raced. He had no idea why.

"I thought you were in such a hurry to get this over with."

He looked up to see Boolkie standing in the doorway with an empty box.

"Um, yeah. Sorry." He got to his feet and made them take him to Papa-Ben's dresser where a mess of old framed photographs competed for space.

Boolkie picked up one with a gilt-edged frame. A corner had crumbled away, making it balance dangerously on the lacy thing that covered the dresser. "Who are they, anyway?"

"His mom and sisters." Cobber's voice sounded raspy.

"Sure is old. When … where was it taken?"

"Russia. After Papa-Ben and his dad left. The others … they never got here."

Boolkie set the photo down and seemed to shrink before Cobber's eyes. "Sorry, man. I-I didn't know."

"It's okay." Cobber tried to *make* it be. He stared at the stern, faded faces of his relatives. Remembered how Papa-Ben and his dad had had it all planned out. They would escape to America, earn enough money, and then send for the women after a few years. But the Russian government had other ideas. That photo was Papa-Ben's and his dad's last look at them. He had to remember them as facts, not feelings. Just had to. "Hey," he said, "did Papa-Ben ever tell you what happened when he first saw the Statue of Liberty?"

Boolkie shook his head.

"He cried. Said she looked just like his mom." Another fact. *Please let it stay another fact.*

"Oy. Poor woman." Boolkie crossed his eyes, and Cobber laughed. Laughed so hard his eyes watered and his knees went weak and he wanted to hug Boolkie for saving him from falling into the big black hole he was trying so carefully to avoid.

"Hey, it wasn't *that* funny," Boolkie said.

Cobber dabbed at his eyes with the bottom of his baggy t-shirt. "Yeah, I know."

"You gonna be all right if I go pack up his bookcase?"

Cobber nodded. Before long, Dad and his friend hustled in and took the old dresser and nightstand.

Alone now in the bedroom, Cobber taped the last box closed and shoved it out into the hall. He turned back for one last look around. All traces of Papa-Ben were gone, the mattress and box springs upended against the wall. Cobber winced at the sight. It was as if Papa-Ben had died, and they were taking care of the remains of his life, his memories, reducing them to identical packages that could be easily ignored or thrown away.

His breathing quickened. Sweat broke out on his neck. All at once, he needed air. Fresh air. Now. Racing past Boolkie, he threw the sliding door open and stepped outside onto the balcony. Immediately, the crisp fall air slapped his burning cheeks, jolting him back. Papa-Ben was *alive*. He was fine. Why was Cobber freaking out? Breathing deeply, he bent forward like a runner at the end of a race. He steadied himself against the railing.

Then Boolkie was at his side. "Jeez, man, are you okay? You gonna hurl?"

Cobber shook his head but did not stand up.

"What's the matter? You want me to get your dad? Look! There he is, down by the truck."

"No, I'm fine."

"Yeah, right."

Cobber ignored his comment. "Are you almost done in there, Boolkie? I-I've just got to get out of here."

"Sit down." Boolkie pulled over Papa-Ben's plastic lounger. "You don't look so good. Want some water or something? Maybe there's some juice in the fridge."

Cobber blinked up at him. "The fridge?" They'd forgotten to empty it. "Oh my gosh, Boolkie, the fridge!" He didn't explain, just hurried to the kitchen. He'd forgotten something else, too—or at least the promise of something. Flinging open the door, he squatted and pulled out the paper sack of tulip bulbs. "What's that? Another lunch in case you toss your first one?"

Cobber offered up a weak laugh and quickly explained. He guessed they'd better load that planter box into the truck, too.

"So, are you okay now?" Boolkie asked, and Cobber could see the worry in his eyes. "You looked like you were going to pass out for a minute there."

"I don't know." Cobber shook his head. "One minute I was packing, and the next, I looked around and it was like … Papa-Ben had died. He was just *gone*, without a trace. And all we had left were boxes."

"Weird."

Cobber's fingers played with the zigzag edge of the paper sack. "You know, I don't think it was like that with my mom," he said finally.

"What do you mean?"

"The boxes. I don't remember anything like that."

"You were little," Boolkie said. "Maybe you forgot."

"Yeah, maybe. But it's not like we had to get rid of her stuff so somebody else could move in. I do remember some things, though."

Boolkie drew closer. "Really?"

"It was quiet, you know, when I woke up? It was like the whole house was still sleeping. But then I heard these strange voices, talking low. And I crept downstairs, wanting Mom, wanting breakfast. And there wasn't any. Just Dad, who wasn't really big or strong anymore. He looked broken. Like one of my old action figures. And then I saw the men. They were wearing the same dark suits, the same dark faces. And then *your* mom was there and she was hugging my dad and they were both crying. Crying! Both of them. And out in the driveway was this white van. A van!"

"Man, that must have been so hard."

"Yep." Cobber blinked quickly, then glanced about the bare kitchen. "I wonder who'll live here next. How long do you think Papa-Ben's smell will last?"

"Until the new guy farts." Boolkie smirked, made google-eyes, and Cobber finally smiled. What would he do without Boolkie here? He'd probably have come unglued by now. "Go sit outside, if you want," Boolkie said. "The fridge is practically empty, and Papa-Ben hardly has any books at all. Just photo albums. I'll be done in a sec."

Dad and his friend bustled in then, ready to get the bed. "Looks like you two have this all under control," Dad said. "Once we load the boxes and get the stuff from outside, I guess that'll about do it. Double-check we have everything, okay, Cobber?"

What could they have missed? Without Papa-Ben, there was nothing here. Nothing of value, anyway. Why couldn't Dad just let him leave already?

Cobber checked around again, though, and finally Dad returned. "Good job, guys. You ready? Come on, then." He turned to his friend. "We'll take most of this stuff and put it in storage," he said. "There's a place over by the mall."

"What about his chair?" Cobber blurted. No way Dad should put *that* in storage.

"The family room's pretty crowded already, don't you think?"

"But it has to feel like *home* to him, not just our family room," he said.

"Cobber, there's no room."

"There *has* to be. You don't want Papa-Ben to feel like a guest, do you?"

Dad raked his fingers through his hair and sighed. "Okay, okay. We'll make it fit somehow. Come on now. We've got to get going. Gotta get the truck back."

Cobber bolted for the door. Finally, *finally*! But at the last second he held back. He had the strangest feeling he'd lived this moment, this leaving, before.

"What?" Boolkie whispered. "I thought you wanted to go."

"I do, but …" A memory flickered through his mind of a musical Dad had taken Papa-Ben and him to see on his tenth birthday. They'd driven all the way to Whitewater and on a school night, too. "Did you ever see *Fiddler on the Roof*?" he asked.

Boolkie shook his head.

"Those people had to leave their homes overnight, just like Papa-Ben."

"So?" Boolkie made a *tsk*ing sound with his tongue. "Man, you're not going to get weird on me again, are you?"

"No. It's just that Papa-Ben cried all through the show, and I didn't understand why. Not then. But I do now."

"Are you guys coming or not?" Dad was already out in the hall. "Get a move on, both of you!"

Boolkie started off after him, but something inexplicable made Cobber hesitate. Again. A kind of whispered reminder in Papa-Ben's own voice, only the words weren't clear. No one else seemed to hear, though. He frowned, but stepped out into the hall with the others. Dad locked the door and headed off toward the elevator with his friend.

Still Cobber stalled.

Boolkie nudged his arm. "What?"

He shrugged, glanced about. A glint of metal caught his eye. The mezuzah! "Dad, wait!" He pointed, feeling suddenly giddy. "Look what we almost forgot!"

"Good eyes, Cobber! Thanks."

Once Dad had pried it from the wall with his pocket-knife, Cobber could see the little scroll of Hebrew verse tucked into the back side. "Can you read *that*?" he teased Boolkie.

"Oh sure. If I had a magnifying glass."

"I'll loan you one of Papa-Ben's, if you come help us unpack."

Dad held the elevator. Cobber's fingers closed around the mezuzah in his pocket. He hurried toward his father and home.

Chapter 15

The next day, after Dad let them out of the car, Papa-Ben paused at the edge of the front walk and seemed to sway like a shriveled corn stalk in a gentle wind. Cobber took Papa-Ben's arm and handed him his cane. "Easy now," he said. "You're almost home."

"Home." Papa-Ben murmured the word like a prayer. His tiny but determined steps finally took them to the front door. Dad had already unlocked it from the inside and now opened it wide in welcome. At the sill, Papa-Ben paused, kissed his fingers, and touched the Sterns' mezuzah. Cobber wondered whether he might want to mount his own inside by his new room.

Papa-Ben's thin shoulders rose and fell beneath his denim jacket. "You do not know, either of you, how grateful I am to … to be here." He looked from Dad to Cobber, and his eyes shone behind his glasses.

Did he mean here at the house, or here, alive? Not that it mattered. "Well, we're grateful, too, Papa-Ben," Cobber said. "Come on. Just wait till you see your room."

Down the front hall and through the kitchen, Papa-Ben *ooh*ed and *aah*ed at everything as if he were in an art gallery. Cobber had never paid much attention to the paintings and needlework panels before, but now, seeing them through Papa-Ben's eyes, they suddenly took on new color and texture and life. It embarrassed him, though, how seldom he and Dad had invited Papa-Ben over. Why did they always visit him at the center or take him out to eat or to a show?

At the entrance to the family room—*his* room—Papa-Ben clutched Cobber's arm. "Oh my God, Yacobe! Such a rainbow you make for me!" When he raised both hands at the *WELCOME PAPA-BEN* computer banner, he looked like the movie version of Moses on Mount Sinai. Cobber was glad he'd spent most of the night before coloring it in with Magic Markers. Glad Dad had helped hang it that morning high above the mantel.

"And all my things ..." Papa-Ben looked around, noting his own bed in one corner, his dresser and green recliner alongside. All that remained of the old family room was the ugly striped sofa, the TV, and VCR. "Come here, both of you."

Dad joined Cobber at Papa-Ben's side. Again, Papa-Ben raised his hands, but this time, one hovered over Cobber's head and the other over Dad's. Then he recited some words in Hebrew that sounded full of awe, like a prayer. Cobber bowed his head, and out of the corner of his eye, saw Dad do the same.

"May the Creator of the sun and the moon and the stars shine upon you, and be gracious unto you. May the Lord bless you and keep you. May He lift up His countenance upon you, and give you peace," Papa-Ben added in translation.

When he finished, Dad's Adam's apple bobbed beneath the roughness of his beard. "Thank you, Papa," he said hoarsely.

Cobber had never been prayed over before, and he didn't know how to react. He shifted his weight, uncomfortable in the silence. Finally, he said, "Hey, um, did you see we got your mail?" He pointed to the bed. "Maybe you want to take your coat off, sit down or something. I could make you some tea."

"Very good, Yacobe." Papa-Ben let Dad help him with the jacket, and handed over his cap. "Tea sounds wonderful!" He shuffled though the slim stack of mail—junk, most of it—and exclaimed over a large white envelope, hand-lettered with calligraphy. "What is this?"

"Open it," Cobber said. "See for yourself." Though he knew what it was—he and Dad had received one just like it the day before—he didn't want to spoil the surprise.

Papa-Ben fumbled with the flap. Finally, he handed it to Dad to slit open with a pocketknife. Carefully he withdrew a shiny red card with black letters down a white strip on the right edge. "Larry, what do you make of this?"

"Just read it." Cobber couldn't wait to see Papa-Ben's reaction to the part where it asked everyone to bring dog food to the temple as part of Eli's mitzvah project.

"Give it here." Dad took the card. "I'll read it."

"He can do it," Cobber said, suddenly indignant for Papa-Ben. Just because he was old, just because he'd gotten out of the hospital, Dad didn't have to treat him like he was helpless.

"It … it is my glasses, Yacobe," Papa-Ben said, glancing over the top of them at Dad. "They are not right, eh?"

The telephone rang then, and Cobber ran to answer it. Mrs. Berman was calling, wanting to know whether she and Eli and Boolkie could come over for a short visit, to see Papa-Ben. "That'd be great," he said. "I'm sure he'd like that. He was just now opening Eli's bar mitzvah invitation."

"Oh, good, because Eli wants to ask him something." She paused. "Cobber, I hear everything's planned out for tomorrow. A caregiver will be there when you're at school."

"That's great. So it's all arranged? I guess Dad called that agency."

"See you in about an hour, then."

By the time Cobber had readied the tea and brought it in on a tray, Papa-Ben had settled into his green recliner, wearing old worn slippers instead of his tennis shoes.

Dad squeezed behind the chair to check the heat vent. "Warm enough for you?" he asked.

"Fine, Larry, wonderful. When my check comes, I want you to—"

"Never mind about that."

"No charity, do you hear me? Ben Kuper pays his way."

Dad nodded, but Cobber had the feeling it was only to prevent an argument.

"I am serious, Larry. You have Yacobe to think of, his college fund, eh? I do not want to be a burden."

Cobber couldn't believe Papa-Ben was already worried about him going to college. He set the tray on the dresser. Then he smoothed the afghan that covered the bed even though there wasn't a wrinkle in sight.

"You could never be a burden, Papa. We love you." Dad patted Papa-Ben's hand. "Don't you know that?"

"But if I should get sick …? Listen, Larry, I am telling you something. If this is too much, me being here, I want you to say so. Do you understand? You have your life to live."

"Really," Dad said, "your moving in, it's a blessing for us."

"Yeah, a mitzvah." Cobber loved the way Papa-Ben's face lit up, hearing him say that word. "It gets lonely being the only one around here."

"So, we will be lonely together, eh?" Papa-Ben smiled and Cobber handed him his tea, steaming hot the way he liked it. He took a long, noisy sip. "Aaah! Perfect, Yacobe. Thank you."

Cobber noticed that Eli's invitation sat atop the dresser now, alongside Papa-Ben's wedding photo. A place of honor. He should have known Papa-Ben would react that way.

"How about some lunch, Papa?" Dad asked. "Man can't live by tea alone. Do you feel up to going into the kitchen? You sit, I'll cook."

He went on ahead, and Cobber halved his steps to stay

back with Papa-Ben. His shuffling walk seemed stiffer than before. Slower, too. And either Cobber had suddenly had a growth spurt or Papa-Ben had shrunk. Maybe it was the slippers. Still, for the first time he realized he didn't have to look up to see Papa-Ben eye to eye. When they finally reached the table, Papa-Ben collapsed into the nearest chair—the one Cobber usually sat in—looking as if he'd just run a mile in under four minutes. Cobber brought his tea in from the family room.

"What would you like, Papa?"

"Anything is fine, Larry. Thank you." Papa-Ben straightened the woven straw placemat, then tucked a paper napkin beneath his chin.

Cobber hesitated before sitting in Mom's chair. Next thing he knew, he was fiddling with the remote control. Lots of times he'd watch MTV or Nickelodeon while he ate, but he doubted that would go down too well with Papa-Ben.

"You don't keep kosher anymore, right?" Dad called from the depths of the refrigerator.

Papa-Ben dismissed the question with a wave of his hand.

"But I thought you were so ..." Cobber swallowed the word *Jewish*.

Papa-Ben tipped Cobber's chin up. "You were saying?"

"Nothing." He avoided his great-grandfather's eyes.

"There are many ways to practice Judaism, Yacobe. What is important is that we practice, yes? That we *can* practice."

"Amen to that," Dad said. "God bless America." Dad, who rarely went to services, even on the High Holy Days.

151

Dad, who worked on Sabbath, complained about temple dues, and ate moo shu pork from Chen Li's.

"Don't look at me that way, young man." Dad waved his spoon at Cobber. A disgusting white glob sailed through the air and landed at Cobber's feet. "And for your information, I am *not* a hypocrite."

"But you *are* a mind reader," Cobber muttered. He tried hard to make his face a mask as he leaned over with a napkin to wipe up the mayonnaise.

"You want to repeat that?" Dad asked. He looked like he had a whole lecture about mouthing off ready to fly.

"Larry, Larry, leave the boy be. He is confused, eh? Let him work it out."

Finally! Someone on *his* side. And how did he repay Papa-Ben? By refusing to have a bar mitzvah. Why couldn't he just make himself do it? For the first time, he tried on the possibility. The heck with bringing dog food to the temple. He'd have people do something more important than *that*. Human beings—little kids, even—were starving, living on the street, right here in Lake Tilton. And Eli picked feeding *dogs* as his mitzvah project?

Cobber shook his head at the stupid fantasy. Riiight. Him, learning Hebrew? Making speeches? Like he'd really go through with it. Even for Papa-Ben. Matter of fact, it was going to take more than magic to keep him from withdrawing from the school talent show.

* * * *

When the Bermans arrived, Boolkie's mother handed Dad a still-steaming, foil-wrapped package that whispered of cinnamon, and Cobber took the boys back to see Papa-Ben. He could hear Dad exclaiming, "Oh, Patty, my favorite! That was so sweet of you," and wondered what special treat she'd brought. Kugel, he hoped. He loved that noodle pudding almost as much as her blintzes. At least it wasn't tongue or chopped liver—which Dad loved—or yucky stuffed cabbage, one of Papa-Ben's favorites.

"Well, here it is." Cobber made a sweeping gesture with his arm. "Home sweet home."

Papa-Ben struggled to get out of his recliner to greet them. Boolkie waved him back. Eli was staring at the WELCOME PAPA-BEN banner. Cobber braced himself for some nasty comment like *What's the matter? Didn't anyone ever teach you to color inside the lines?* He had a way of treating Cobber like a real brother sometimes. Insults and all.

"So," Papa-Ben said, nodding in Eli's direction, "this is the bar mitzvah boy, eh?"

Eli seemed to grow a couple of inches before their eyes. Finally he looked taller than his "little" brother Boolkie. Or maybe it was just his out-of-control hair, which was sure to be gone by bar mitzvah day.

"You should hear him, Papa-Ben," Boolkie said. "He's going to *chant*. Oy. Such a voice!"

Eli glared at his brother. But given the way Eli's voice *had* been cracking lately, Cobber was sure Boolkie wasn't exaggerating. Why had he chosen to *sing* the Hebrew rather than just say it? "Don't worry about me," Eli said at last. "I'll be okay. God will help me."

Oh, please. Get off it, Eli. Cobber rolled his eyes, and noticed that Boolkie did, too.

But Papa-Ben was eating up every word. "You are right, Elijah. He *will* help you."

Eli turned to Cobber and smirked. "Nice rainbow." He indicated the banner. "Did you make it in my honor?"

"No." Can't you read, dummy?

"Betcha don't even know when rainbows started," Eli said. "Or why."

"What kind of a question is that?" Cobber asked.

Eli only shrugged. "Listen good at my bar mitzvah and maybe you'll find out."

Cobber scowled, certain Eli was just showing off for Papa-Ben, trying to look like Mr. Big, Mr. Know-it-all. Trying to make Cobber look bad. "I thought you had something you wanted to ask him," he said, suddenly impatient for Eli, in particular, to go. "I thought it was so important."

"It *is* important, actually." Eli approached Papa-Ben and knelt beside the recliner. What was he going to do? Propose? "I see you got my invitation."

Papa-Ben nodded. "November fourth, eh? I have it on my social calendar."

Good old Papa-Ben. Cobber grinned.

"I was wondering if you would accept an aliyah—the seventh," Eli said, his voice low.

"Elijah, such an honor!" Papa-Ben's cheeks seemed to pink right up at the very idea. "Are you sure you want *me*?"

"Absolutely."

By this time, Dad and Mrs. Berman had come in from the kitchen. Cobber could feel them behind him, taking in the whole thing.

"Patty, was this your idea?" Dad whispered. "Look how pleased he is. It will give him something to get stronger for. Something to look forward to."

Cobber couldn't hear her reply. Suddenly his ears weren't working right. They went hot along with his cheeks. A strange pressure started building in his chest. All he could hear was this little kid, stomping around inside his head, yelling for Papa-Ben to *look at me, look at me* that way, too.

Chapter 16

"So, class," Mrs. Kelso said Monday morning, "how are you coming along on your family history projects? First drafts are due next week, remember."

Megan O'Brien's hand shot up. She asked if there was a way to get extra credit. Like she really needed it. After Boolkie, she was the best writer in the class. But Cobber, on the other hand, could use all the extra credit he could get. He straightened in his chair, set his pencils out—one, two, three—and fingered the newly sharpened tips.

"You know what would interest me?" Mrs. Kelso paused, as if someone might actually try to guess. "Hearing from your sources first hand. In their own voices. If any of you have older relatives who'd like to share their stories with the class, I'd be glad to award extra credit."

Cobber looked around to see whether this news interested everyone else as much as it did him. He caught Megan looking back at him. Smiling. Like she could read his thoughts. Like she knew something about him but wasn't telling. He forced his lips upward, though the rest of his face was frowning.

Mrs. Kelso approached the blackboard, chalk in hand, firing off a list of reminders about what the project was supposed to include. Immediately, Megan turned forward and Cobber could see the eraser end of her yellow pencil dance.

His thoughts turned to Papa-Ben. He'd be perfect for extra credit. Mrs. Kelso was going to love his stories about escaping Russia as a little kid and going to work in those sweat shops in New York City. His accent, even the Yiddish words he sometimes used—he'd be great! Cobber could just hear Mr. Olson, their social studies teacher, now: "A perfect example of the early-twentieth-century immigrant who made America what it is today." Papa-Ben would be like a boring history book come to life.

"Okay, then," Mrs. Kelso said. "See me after class if you want to schedule a day for your source to come talk."

Cobber made a mental note not to rush off with Boolkie to Basic Survival. As much as he secretly looked forward to that class, today cooking and sewing would have to wait. Boolkie could joke around all he wanted, but Cobber never knew when *he'd* need to know those things. Maybe he'd learn how to cook something for Papa-Ben—surprise him and Dad with a whole dinner one of these days. He wondered what he might make ...

"Pssst, Cobber!" Boolkie pointed to a triangle of note-paper that the kid in front of Cobber was trying to pass back.

His pulse raced as he took the note. It was from a girl. Had to be. No guy would think of doing Japanese paper-folding to keep something private. Gently, he unwrapped the triangle and, taking care not to make any noise, hid the paper in his folder. Then he peeked inside to read it:

> *C (J), I need to talk to you!*
> *Wait for me after class, k?*
> *MOB*

Megan O'Brien wanted to talk to *him*? He couldn't imagine why. And what was with the J in parentheses? Weird, all of it. Across the aisle, Boolkie was frowning, waiting for an explanation, but Cobber only shrugged.

When the bell rang at last, he told Boolkie he'd meet him in Basic Survival. Then he approached Mrs. Kelso, seated at her desk. She looked up from a stack of papers. "Jacob?"

"I'd like my great-grandfather to come sometime. You know, for extra credit."

"*Great*-grandfather?"

He nodded. "He's almost a hundred, but his memory's good." *About some things.* "You should hear all the stuff he remembers about Russia—dirt floors, this big fireplace in the middle of his house, raids on their village."

A wide smile lit Mrs. Kelso's face. "What a unique perspective he has, Jacob! Let's schedule him for next week, okay? How about Monday?"

Cobber scribbled the date in ink on the back of his hand. There. That'd give Papa-Ben something else besides Eli's stupid bar mitzvah to put on his social calendar.

He hurried off to meet Megan. She was waiting in the hall, her book bag slung over one shoulder. For some reason, the lighting out here made her reddish hair fade to a fiery blonde that bounced about and brushed her shoulders. He licked his lips and wished he could wet his dry throat as easily.

"Megan?" He could barely get her name out.

She turned, fingering a tiny gold heart that nestled in the hollow of her neck. "Oh, good. I was afraid you were trying to avoid me."

"No. Just getting a time for my great-grandfather to come in."

"Oh, goodie! I hoped you'd do that." When she grinned, a dimple creased each cheek. "My mom told me what happened. He's okay, isn't he?"

Cobber nodded. "How did *she* find out?" Jeez, had Papa-Ben's accident made the front page or something?

"She works at the center. Didn't you know that? She's the activity director."

"Oh. Well. Papa-Ben isn't exactly big on balloon volleyball or bridge."

"I know." Megan sighed. "Mom said she could hardly ever budge him out of his room. He was always waiting for 'his Yacobe.'"

Cobber eyed his shoes. Was she making fun of Papa-Ben's accent? Would the other kids? "I—we'd better go or we'll be late." He started toward his next class, unsure whether Megan's was on the way. But she stuck right with him.

"Boolkie says you're going to be in the talent show."

"Um, well, I signed up for it but I …" He shrugged helplessly.

"Jacob Stern, you are *not* going to chicken out, are you? I mean, magic is so cool, and I know you'll be great."

"Wish *I* did," he said. Where did she and Boolkie get such confidence in him? Didn't she still remember third grade?

Her gaze softened, and his knees went weak. "You are not that little kid anymore," she said gently. So she *did* remember. "Mom says, 'If you think you can or you think you can't, you're right, either way.'"

Cobber thought about that for a moment. He wondered if she had a point, if it was simply a matter of changing another attitude.

"Please," she begged, batting those long eyelashes at him. "Will you do it for *me*?"

Cobber's throat went dry. His pulse quickened. Words wouldn't come, even though he would have written a rhyming poem for her had she asked.

"Is that a yes? Do you promise?"

At last he nodded weakly, swallowed hard.

"Just imagine everyone in their underwear. That's what my mom tells *me*. And I'll sit in the very first row, cheering you on."

Your mom is just full of great advice. "O-Okay," he managed. It felt like he was stepping off the tallest building into thin air.

"Goodie!" Megan clapped her hands. "But actually, that's not what I wanted to talk to you about, Jacob," she said, her voice getting breathier. Maybe he was walking too fast. "I *can* call you Jacob, can't I? Cobber's so—I don't know—babyish, I guess. I mean, we *are* in middle school."

"Yeah, but Cobber's . . ." How could he explain it was *Mom's* name for him, that giving it up was like giving *her* up, forever? "Never mind. Jacob's fine, I guess. It *is* my name, isn't it?"

"Good." She giggled. "It's about the bar mitzvah."

"Eli Berman's?"

"Yes, our whole family's invited."

"Really?"

"My dad and Mr. Berman play tennis together, and my sister's a friend of Eli's."

Cobber glanced at his watch, wished she'd get on with this. They were going to be late. And what did any of this have to do with *him*?

"I-I just wondered if I could call you sometime—you know—to talk and stuff. About the bar mitzvah, I mean. I've never been to one, and I figured you could kind of, like, fill me in."

That's funny, Megan. I haven't actually been to one either. "Oh, sure," he said. "Call me any time."

"Is your whole family going? Your great-grandpa, too?"

"He's supposed to. He's got an aliyah." Dumb. Like she would really know what *that* was.

She frowned, and her eyebrows knit together in a thin strand of gold. "See what I mean? I *need* you, Jacob."

Oh, boy. His pulse quickened. "It's when somebody comes forward to bless the Torah. It's a big deal, an honor, really."

"Oh, I see. Thanks." Megan giggled again, and her grin made his stomach flip over on itself. "By the time *you* get bar mitzvah'd, I'll be a real pro."

"Um, yeah." He stopped outside his classroom. "I guess you will." He hoped she wouldn't hate him when she never got an invitation.

"Don't forget your promise," she said, turning to go. "Practice up. I just *know* you're going to be amazing."

* * * *

"Papa-Ben, I'm home!" Cobber yelled from the front hall. "How was your day?" *Listen to me. I sound just like Dad.* He dropped his backpack and headed for the family room.

A lady wearing teal pajama-looking clothes rose from the sofa to greet him. According to a company badge, her name was Debbie. "He's had a good day. Ate well at lunch, too. Napped for a while. Do you have any questions? Will you be okay if I leave now?"

Cobber nodded and thanked her.

"And what about you, Yacobe?" Papa-Ben reached up from his recliner to give Cobber a hug. He smelled faintly of spaghetti sauce, and when Cobber looked closer, he noticed a red smear on his chin. He debated whether to do the old spit-on-the-finger trick—like Mom did when he was little—to clean it off. No doubt Papa-Ben would hate that as much as he had. "So, come. We will have some tea."

Papa-Ben set out the cups, spoons, tea bags, and sugar, while Cobber put the kettle on. Glimpsing the back of his hand, he said, "Oh, shoot. I almost forgot to tell you my good news."

Papa-Ben leaned heavily on the table, then lowered himself into the nearest chair. "So tell already. I am not getting any younger."

Cobber grinned and explained about the extra credit, asking Papa-Ben whether he would go to school on Monday. "You'll save my grade," he said. "I just know it."

Papa-Ben rubbed his hands together, avoiding Cobber's eyes. At last he let out a great sigh. "Oh, Yacobe, please do not ask this of me."

"But … *why*? You said yourself that good grades are important."

"Yes, I did. But you must earn them, not get them as gifts. Your teacher, she is a *meshuggeneh*, you should pardon the expression."

Where did he get off calling Mrs. Kelso crazy? "She is not, Papa-Ben," he said. "She just gives you a break, that's all."

"Then please, Yacobe, you give *me* a break. How can I do this thing you are asking? I know from nothing."

The kettle began to squeal. Cobber turned the stove off and poured the hot water. Maybe tea would calm Papa-

Ben. It wasn't as if Cobber were asking him to talk about somebody *else's* life.

"You don't have to give a speech," he said. "Just tell your stories, like you do with me."

"You are family. With you, I can talk."

"But …" Cobber's voice trailed off, and it occurred to him for the first time that maybe Papa-Ben was as nervous about talking in front of a group as he was. Well, he could read, then. Cobber had already written down some of his stories for the history project. "I have an idea," he said. "Wait here. I'll be right back."

Upstairs, he printed off his interview pages and then brought them back to the table. "Look! All you've got to do is *read*."

Without even glancing at them, Papa-Ben set the pages aside. "I am sorry, Yacobe. This, I cannot do."

Sudden heat flared in Cobber's cheeks. *And they say I'm stubborn!* "Can't or won't?" His father's expression flew from his mouth.

Papa-Ben looked into his cup as if the answer were there in the non-existent tea leaves. "Can't," he said softly.

"But …"

Papa-Ben raised his eyes, watering now, to meet Cobber's. They were like huge blue oceans behind his thick glasses. "Can't, Yacobe."

Cobber's mouth opened and closed. What? Not know how to read? Impossible. Papa-Ben had lived here most of his life. Worked here, too. But all his excuses—and Dad's, too—came reeling back. Cobber wondered how he could have missed all those clues. "I-I'm sorry, Papa-Ben," he said at last. "I didn't know. I never realized."

"And why should you? I wanted it that way. It is shame enough that Larry knows."

"But why didn't you ever learn? You're smart. You can even read Hebrew. I've seen you."

"Yes, that is true. But school? I never went. I worked, eh? From the time I was a little boy. One day my father, he sent me to night school. Unlucky for me, my cousin was the teacher." Papa-Ben looked around the kitchen, at everything but Cobber.

"So, why didn't you stay?"

"Ah, Yacobe, I was so ashamed of my English, that my cousin should hear. *Tschut, tschut.* Maybe with a stranger, I would stay. But I was foolish. Too proud. I wish my father had made me try again." Papa-Ben sighed as if the effort of dragging up the memory exhausted him.

"But it's not like you *couldn't* learn," Cobber said firmly.

"Of course I learned. I learned to sew, I went to *shul*, studied for my bar mitzvah, took care of my family—that was my life, eh?"

"No, I mean now. Hey! Maybe I could teach you."

Papa-Ben did not reply. Instead, he sipped his tea and made a face like a prune. "More hot water, please." He slid the cup toward Cobber. "You have a good heart, Yacobe. I am sure of that. But I am an old man. It is too late for me now, but it is not too late for you."

"What's that supposed to mean?" Cobber couldn't stand the way Papa-Ben was talking, like his brain was dead, like his life was over. "Look, how about this? We'll make a deal. I teach you English and … and … you teach me Hebrew."

Where the idea came from, Cobber had no clue. He held his breath, waiting for Papa-Ben to say something. Anything. Was it really so crazy—their teaching each other?

At last, Papa-Ben nodded. "Okay by me. But I am telling you, Yacobe, a teacher I am not."

"Well, that goes double for me. All we can do is try." He couldn't help but grin. "So, when do you want to start?"

Papa-Ben shrugged. "I will let you know, eh?"

"Fine. And Papa-Ben?" Cobber lowered his voice as if the dust bunnies in the corners had real ears. "Can we keep this just between us, you know, in case … well, it doesn't work out?"

"Even better, Yacobe." Papa-Ben winked. "It is a deal, then."

Chapter 17

That night for dinner, Dad brought home Chinese. But Papa-Ben only grimaced at the mess of green peppers, maraschino cherries, pineapple, and fried chicken. Instead of eating, he watched the steam rise from his bowl of wonton soup.

Cobber wondered what he was thinking about, why he wouldn't eat, and squirmed in his seat. This was not the happy family gathering he had imagined. Dad wasn't talking either, but at least he wasn't reading the paper. That was one good thing. Cobber searched for something to say, something that would make them both perk up. Smile. But he came up empty.

"Bob called today," Dad said at last.

Papa-Ben sighed. "So. What is new with the Kaddish *Kind*?"

"What's that mean?" Cobber asked. "Not Kaddish. The other thing. 'Kint.'"

"That's what my dad—your Grandpa Jacob—used to call my brother," Dad said. "He was the extra son, the insurance policy that there'd be at least one male to say Kaddish at Dad's funeral."

"Ha." Papa-Ben took a long swallow of tea.

Cobber wondered whether Papa-Ben's reaction had something to do with Uncle Bob marrying Aunt Laura and bringing their kids up Catholic.

"To answer your question, Papa, Bob's fine. He said to send his love."

Papa-Ben nodded mechanically. "So, who is going to be *my* Kaddish *Kind*, eh?" He looked from Dad to Cobber, then down at his soup again.

A lump rose in Cobber's throat. He wanted to eat double-time, but knew he'd never be able to swallow.

"When the time comes, Papa," Dad said gently, "someone will be there to say it. Don't worry."

Papa-Ben just shrugged. Cobber stared at the mess of food on his plate—reds and yellows and greens all jumbled together—and wished they'd both get off the subject. Papa-Ben's time wasn't coming for a while yet. They still had things to do. Plant those tulip bulbs in the backyard. Watch them come up in the spring, together.

"So, Papa, you want to go to temple on *Shabbos*?" Dad asked.

Good for him, Cobber thought.

"Isn't it also Erev Rosh Hashanah?" Dad continued. "Cobber brought home a note about it from Sunday school, but I forget."

"Yes, of course, Larry. If it is no trouble. Maybe you and Yacobe will come too, eh?"

"Maybe," Dad answered for himself and Cobber both.

Cobber resigned himself to spending Friday night and Saturday, too, at temple. With the Jewish New Year not falling on a school day, he had pretty much lost his usual excuse for not going to daytime services. *Suck it up and change your attitude*, a little voice whispered. Cobber accepted a prick of guilt. God had come through big time for Papa-Ben, hadn't He? The least Cobber could do was show some thanks. Besides, he reminded himself, Boolkie and his family would be there, too. The Bermans might keep the deli open on Saturdays, ignoring Sabbath, but they'd absolutely close on Rosh Hashanah. "Not maybe," he said at last. "I'm going for sure."

"Good." Papa-Ben blotted his lips with his napkin, then sighed, pushing his soup bowl away. Untouched. His eyes lost their focus as he gazed off across the room.

Cobber nudged his hand. "Are you all right?"

Papa-Ben shrugged. "A *fresser*, I am not."

"No one says you have to be a *big* eater," Dad said, "but you do have to eat *something*. How else are you going to get your strength back?"

"I am not hungry, Larry. What can I tell you?"

"If Grandma had made it, you'd be hungry." Dad reached across the table to push the soup closer. "Her chicken soup? You loved that."

"Ya, ya."

Riiiight. Big difference between Great-Grandma's soup and take-out Chinese.

"She was a great cook, Grandma Dvosha." Dad's face

had a dreamy little-kid look that Cobber had never seen before. "Remember how she used to make *Shabbos* every week, Papa? We'd all get together. Feels like a lifetime ago."

"Two," Papa-Ben corrected, "but what can you do?"

Cobber imagined what it must have been like when Dad was a kid—him, Uncle Bob, Aunt Gail, their parents, and his Stern grandparents gathering every Friday night at Papa-Ben's and Great-Grandma Dvosha's apartment. Three generations in one tiny space, all scrunched together around the table. Definitely more exciting than *this* family dinner was turning out to be. "Dad, do you ... need a woman around, to do that—to make *Shabbos*?" he asked at last.

"Why, no, I guess not." Dad looked to Papa-Ben. "It's just that there's a lot to do—set a nice table, cook, that kind of thing. Grandma used to make it real special, somehow. She'd bake fresh challah every week, remember, Papa?"

"Ya, ya," Papa-Ben said again, and seemed to sink even further into his chair, the one Cobber had always sat in before he moved over into Mom's. "I loved her chicken, too."

"*Roasted* chicken?" Dad said.

Papa-Ben shook his head. "No. Boiled."

"I remember. Just ... boiled. With vegetables."

Cobber couldn't understand why Dad was scrunching up his face, but Papa-Ben, lost in his memories, seemed not to notice.

Now, sitting where she sat, he could feel Papa-Ben's longing for Great-Grandma, because he still missed Mom that way, too. But the family as it used to be, the old traditions—*those* he couldn't get a feel for by just hearing about them. If only there were a way to make memories like that for himself! What would it take to surprise Papa-Ben and make *Shabbos* for them all?

Cobber imagined his great-grandfather's face, how proud he'd be. Maybe there'd be answers in Mom's notebook, the denim-covered one stuffed full of old Cohen family recipes. For sure she'd have challah in there. And how hard could boiled chicken and vegetables be? Maybe Boolkie could come over and help make it, make the whole Sabbath dinner, for that matter. Cobber could fancy up the dining room table with all Mom's good dishes, the ones they looked at but never touched. He imagined the joy on Dad's face. On Papa-Ben's. It would be great. The real family dinner he'd been dreaming of. He could hardly wait to call Boolkie and make plans. Maybe he'd get that Ouija board out again, tell Mom, and ask her advice, too.

* * * *

After dinner on Thursday, Boolkie's mother dropped him off at Cobber's house, along with all the stuff they'd need for the challah and for making dinner the next day. "Don't come in the kitchen now," Cobber told Dad and Papa-Ben, "or else you'll spoil my surprise."

He handed Boolkie the recipe and turned on the oven so it would be good and hot. "You read, I'll mix, okay?"

"Roger, wilco," Boolkie said. "Yeast?"

"Yeast."

"Sugar?"

"Sugar."

"Lukewarm water?"

"Got it running," Cobber said, turning on the faucet.

While Boolkie held his hands up—*What did he think they were, doctors scrubbing in for surgery?*—Cobber measured the water and the sugar into a bowl and added the yeast. It dissolved in an instant and started to bubble.

Boolkie put flour into another bowl, and Cobber poured in the yeasty water. "What's next?" he asked.

"Salt, shortening, more sugar, and more warm water."

Cobber checked the amounts and dumped them all in.

"Now for the fun part." Boolkie stretched his fingers as if he were about to play the piano. "The gooshing."

Obviously he'd seen his mom do this before, so Cobber followed his lead. Before they knew it, they had both squeezed their hands into the bowl and squooshed them around until all the ingredients came together in a ball.

"I think that's good," Boolkie said at last. "Now put it in another bowl and cover it with a towel."

"Sheesh. How many bowls do you think we have?" Cobber muttered, settling on a metal one Dad used for popcorn. "Now what?"

Boolkie squinted at the faded handwriting. Cobber felt a pang. Even *that* trace of Mom was disappearing. "I think it says to set it in a warm place to rise for forty minutes," Boolkie said, finally.

"We're going to be here all night at this rate." Cobber sighed. "Maybe we should put it in a hot place for half the time."

Boolkie shrugged. "You're the math genius." He opened the oven and slid the bowl in while Cobber set the timer.

Then they waited. And waited. When the phone rang, Cobber jumped up to answer it, joking, "Saved by the bell."

"Jacob? Hi! It's me, Megan. Whatcha doing? Practicing?"

It's Megan, he mouthed to Boolkie, who sidled up to press his ear against the phone. "No, nothing like that." No way he was going to tell her they were baking!

"Um, so, you said you'd tell me all about bar mitzvahs."

Cobber nudged Boolkie with his elbow. Talking to Megan was hard enough without *him* listening in. "What … what do you want to know?" He wished his heart would stop slamming against his ribs. Surely, she'd hear.

"Somebody said you have to wear a hat or something, and, well, I'm not exactly a hat person, so I didn't know—"

"You don't. I mean, girls don't." Jeez. He sounded like an idiot. "There's a box of yarmulkes there, if your dad wants to wear one. You know, out of respect and all. But since you're not Jewish …" His voice trailed off, and his nostrils flared at the strange smell that was suddenly escaping the oven. "Hold on a minute, Megan, will you?"

Cobber set the phone down, grabbed a potholder, and rushed to rescue the bread dough.

"Call her back," Boolkie whispered.

"Hey, Megan, I-I've got to go. It's sort of an emergency. Nothing serious, I mean, but, well, can I call you later?"

Megan giggled. "Yes, Jacob. If you *can*, you *may* call me later."

He rolled his eyes as he hung up the phone. Boolkie shot him a questioning look, but he only shrugged. "Who knows? Something about the bar mitzvah. She's weird." He studied the bread dough, pushing thoughts of Megan from his mind and holding his promise to her close. "Test it, Boolk," he said. "Stick your finger in, like it says."

Boolkie did, and it *kind of* left a hole. They both agreed it had passed the test. As they worked the dough into two braids and set one on top of the other, Cobber realized the stuff was a lot stickier than he had expected. Surely the challah would turn out fine once they baked it. Still, as they peeled it off the floured board and put it on the baking sheet, Cobber's heart thumped faster.

Boolkie covered the loaf with a towel and said they had to let it rise again. This time they left it on top of the stove for thirty minutes.

Boolkie wrinkled up his nose. "This stuff really does stink, doesn't it?"

"It's not so bad," Cobber lied. "Bread always smells best when you bake it, right?"

"It better. Or else we're gonna need a toxic waste permit."

No way. This was going to work. It'd be perfect. Cobber imagined Papa-Ben's face and Dad's when they realized his surprise was making *Shabbos*. Making a new family memory, with a little help from Mom.

Once the challah was in the oven, Boolkie asked about

dinner for the next day. Should he come by after school to help? Cobber told him he planned to boil a chicken, cut up some carrots and potatoes. That sounded easy enough, and Papa-Ben had mentioned Great-Grandma used to make that for Sabbath dinner all the time. It was sure to be a hit.

"Sounds like you won't need me, then," Boolkie said.

Cobber shrugged. He'd know for sure once he was in the middle of it. "How about you go on standby?"

"Roger, wilco." Boolkie gave him a brisk salute.

While the challah was baking, he kept bugging Cobber to call Megan back. He tried five times, but the line was always busy.

Cobber wasn't sure when he first realized it, but little by little, another weird odor stole over the kitchen. It smelled vaguely familiar. He screwed his face up, trying to place it. "Smells like beer."

Boolkie shook his head. "No way. It smells exactly like Eli's dirty feet."

"Gross!" Cobber shuddered. Surely it would taste better than it smelled. They'd worked so hard on it. And what was *Shabbos* without fresh-baked challah? When the buzzer went off at last, they each grabbed a potholder, exchanged a nervous glance, and opened the oven door.

All Cobber could do was stare. What was supposed to be a great, golden twist-bread lay there in the dim oven light like a dark, lumpy stone.

Boolkie clapped a hand on his shoulder. "Never fear. Ma Berman is near."

But Cobber shook his head. Sure, she'd come running and bring a nice perfect challah from the deli. But he didn't want her help. The whole point was doing it himself—and not needing anyone else to pull it off.

"You sure, Cobber? She'd be glad to help. You know she would. What's the difference?"

Cobber sighed. Maybe he *was* stubborn. Or too proud, like Papa-Ben. "I don't know. It's the principle of the thing—that we tried. And don't say *principles, schminciples* again, either."

"We tried all right." Boolkie shrugged. "Suit yourself. I just hope Papa-Ben has an extra set of dentures."

Cobber scowled. Boolkie might be right, but he didn't want to hear it. A Sabbath dinner didn't have to be *perfect*, did it? If God cared at all about the honor-the-Sabbath-and-keep-it-holy commandment, He'd be grateful a kid like Cobber was even trying to make this happen. And so would Dad and Papa-Ben.

Chapter 18

On Friday, Cobber told Mrs. Kelso that Papa-Ben wasn't going to be able to visit their class after all. He eyed the floor and made some excuse about Papa-Ben not feeling up to it. "It's all right, Jacob," she said. "The door's always open."

When he got home, the house was too quiet. The caregiver wasn't even there. A note from Dad explained why. He had taken Papa-Ben for a follow-up visit with the doctor, nothing to worry about, be back soon. Grateful to have some unexpected time alone to ready his surprise, Cobber raced into action. Nipping at the back of his mind was his mother's most recent Ouija board message: WN Good-bye. What in the world did *that* mean? After trying all the vowels—*wan, wen, win, won, wun*—he decided he'd think about it later.

First, he threw a whole chicken; some cut-up, peeled potatoes; and stubby carrots into a pot of water. Turning the burner on HIGH, he set the dinner on to boil. Three hours ought to do it. He knew chicken had to be thoroughly cooked. Wouldn't want anyone getting sick.

Next he washed and tore up lettuce for a salad, sliced a sick-looking tomato, and hunted down some croutons.

The final challenge was to make the dining room look special. He found a lacy white tablecloth in the linen closet, then folded light blue napkins into fans like he'd seen on TV. Getting his hands on some decent flowers was another thing altogether. At last, he rescued a couple of shaggy, brown-edged chrysanthemums from the front flowerbed and floated them in a fancy crystal bowl. He supposed the last person who'd touched it was Mom. He smiled at the thought.

From the china cabinet, he carefully pulled out pale-blue porcelain—three plates and three bowls—with little white birds on the rim. The pieces looked so fragile, he was afraid one sneeze might shatter them to bits. No wonder Dad hadn't used them before. On the highest shelf, he spotted the family Kiddush cup and candlesticks, black with neglect. He swallowed hard. Somehow he had to polish them until they shone like new.

When dish soap and cleanser didn't work, he broke down and called Mrs. Berman. "Oh, help. How do you get the black stuff off?"

She offered to bring him some silver polish.

He hesitated but finally decided that this kind of help didn't qualify as not doing it himself. "Okay, sure. Thanks, Mrs. B."

"You got everything else? Candles? Wine?"

What kind of candles did he need? And where was *he* going to get wine? *Wine*! Was that what Mom meant by WN?

"I take it that's a no," she said, and he could hear the smile in her voice. "No problem. I'll be over in a jiff, okay? Anything else you need?"

He thought about mentioning the challah, then wondered whether Boolkie already had. But something else was tugging at the back of his brain. "Maybe. I'm not sure." Probably, he'd learned the blessings in Sunday school without even trying. Years and years of repetition at monthly "practice services" had a way of magically filing things away in a person's mind. But what if he got tongue-tied and couldn't think of the right words? Boolkie would help—he knew that—but it would be too embarrassing admitting to him that he didn't know even these most basic things. "What if ... do you think I could call Eli about the blessings?" he asked at last. Who cared if *Eli* thought he was an idiot? That went hand-in-hand with being Boolkie's best friend.

"Stage fright, huh?"

"Yeah," he admitted. "Something like that."

"Don't worry about it," she said. "He'd be glad to help, I'm sure. And Boolkie would, too. I hope you know your mom is so proud of what you're doing, honey."

Is. Present tense again. "I hope so," he said, his voice suddenly raspy.

Soon Dad and Papa-Ben came home, complaining about all the people hacking their lungs out in the doctor's waiting room. "It's a wonder the whole world's not sick. They ought to make them wear masks," Dad said. "You go lie down now, Papa. Rest. It's been a long afternoon."

Papa-Ben managed a weak wave to Cobber, then shuffled off to his room.

"Is he okay?" Cobber whispered.

"He's fine." But Dad seemed awfully busy suddenly, emptying his pockets and arranging coins on the counter.

"Fine? That's it?"

"For as old as he is, he's as fine as can be expected, Cobber. He's just … slowing down, that's all. I … I guess I don't like to think about it." He rubbed his eyes, then turned, sniffing the air. "Got dinner cooking, huh? Good going. Looks like that Basic Survival class is paying off. Call me if you need anything. I'll be in my study."

Why was he changing the subject?

With the chicken boiling away and the lid tittering like crazy, Cobber staked out a place by the front door. When Mrs. Berman arrived a few minutes later, she was carrying a brown paper bag.

"What's all that?"

"Here"—she pushed her way past him into the kitchen—"let me show you." She pulled out a bottle of Concord grape wine, two short white candles, a squatty blue-lidded jar, and a covered metal container. "A little something extra." She smiled, turned the oven on, and slid the pan in.

"May I see?" she asked, lifting the lid on the chicken. "Ah, soup. Mind if I taste?"

Cobber shrugged. He hadn't thought he was making soup.

"Okay if I season it a bit?"

"Sure. Why not?"

She salted and peppered the contents, sprinkled in some other spices, and finally turned down the heat. "Don't forget to strain it and pick out the bones," she said, laying a colander and a soup tureen out on the counter.

Since sundown was coming faster than he had expected, he welcomed her offer of help with the silver. While they rubbed at those pieces, he kept sneaking sideways glances at her, trying to imagine his own mother at the sink, doing the same thing. A lump rose in his throat and he looked away. Mom's pressed wildflowers caught the waning light. He squinted hard against the glare.

Before Mrs. Berman left, she slipped Cobber an index card. On it, Eli had written out the blessings over the candles, the wine, and the bread.

If she'd seen the pitiful challah, she didn't let on. He felt relieved to finally hide the ugly thing under a napkin and set it on the table, along with the newly shiny Kiddush cup and candlesticks. Something was missing. A bread knife. He wondered where Dad had stashed the box with Papa-Ben's. Down in the basement, he hoped.

It took some doing to find the right carton. At least they'd labeled them. Papa-Ben would really perk up when he saw that knife again, especially laid out next to a challah Cobber had made himself.

There. Everything was ready, and judging from the fading light outside, just in time, too. He knocked on Dad's door. "Dinner! We've got to hurry."

In the family room, Papa-Ben was sitting on his bed, buttoning up his white shirt for temple. "Ah, Yacobe, smell!" He inhaled deeply and smiled. A sweet, tomato-y aroma, something like spaghetti sauce, snaked out of the kitchen. Whatever Mrs. Berman had put in the oven, Papa-Ben seemed to recognize as something familiar and dear.

"Come on," Cobber said. "You can finish dressing later, okay?"

"God forbid we should be late to supper, eh?" Papa-Ben raised one eyebrow, but Cobber said nothing, holding his surprise close. After stopping to wash his hands, Papa-Ben followed Cobber into the dining room. "Oh my *Gott*!" he cried, and grabbed Cobber's arm. "Larry, come look! The *boychik* made *Shabbos*!" His eyes welled and he pulled Cobber toward him, hugging long and hard.

Cobber could feel each bone of Papa-Ben's rib cage as he rubbed Papa-Ben's back. And though he strained to see Dad's reaction, his great-grandfather's arms held him fast. By the time Papa-Ben let go, Dad was seated at the end farthest from the candlesticks and Kiddush cup. As if he wanted no part of this, them, anything they were about to do as a family.

Cobber's eyes went hot. He tried to tell himself what mattered most was Papa-Ben and *his* reaction. Dad was Dad. Maybe he was never going to change. Could Cobber adjust his attitude to *that*? "Want me to light the candles?" he asked finally.

"You?" The word flew from Dad's mouth.

"Larry, *luz!*" Papa-Ben snapped.

Cobber's back stiffened at the hard edge to Papa-Ben's command. He'd never before heard him tell Dad to be quiet like that, like he—Papa-Ben—was the head of the household. The family.

"I-I'm sorry, Cobber," Dad said. "I didn't mean that like it sounded. You just … surprised me is all. It's always the woman who does that blessing."

"Yeah, well." Cobber raised one shoulder.

"Go on, Yacobe," Papa-Ben said, handing him the matches. "Judaism can be flexible."

Cobber lighted the candles. The bright flames made his eyes water as he read the blessing, pronouncing the Hebrew words the way Eli had written them out in English.

When he finished, Papa-Ben puckered up his lips and sent an invisible kiss off in Cobber's direction. "Larry, you say Kiddush." He passed Dad the filled goblet.

"Are you sure *you* don't want the honor?" Dad asked.

Cobber glared at him across the long table. Why couldn't he *read* the prayer if he didn't remember it?

Papa-Ben shook his head. "This is your house, Larry. *You* are the papa here."

Dad only shrugged, accepting the cup. Then, without hesitation, he recited the blessing over the wine. Perfectly, and in Hebrew. Cobber gaped in disbelief at his father, while Papa-Ben sang along in a haunting melody. "Aaaamen!" they finished together, leaving Cobber out.

He couldn't believe Dad remembered *everything*—and

on the spur of the moment, too. The prayer was just *there*—even after years of not having said it. Amazing.

Dad sipped from the cup, then gave it back to Papa-Ben, who offered Cobber a taste, too. He hesitated—at the Bermans' he always had grape juice—but when Dad nodded his approval, Cobber raised the rim to his lips. The wine was as thick and sweet as the Welch's juice he was used to, but with the punch of cough syrup. He quickly handed the goblet back to Dad.

Cobber knew what came next—the challah—and his heart hammered at the thought. He wished it were golden and soft and perfect. He wished so hard, he knew he could only be disappointed. Still, it was all he had. Slowly, he lifted the napkin.

Papa-Ben's face froze into the "Comedy" mask, the one pictured alongside "Tragedy" in their *Fiddler on the Roof* theater program. "My goodness, Yacobe," he said finally. "Such a challah I have never seen."

"Did you make this?" Dad asked.

"Boolkie and I did. All by ourselves. We used Mom's recipe. Probably, it tastes better than it looks." Yeah, right. Who was he kidding?

"And my knife!" The Sabbath candles shone in Papa-Ben's eyes. "This is *wonderful*, Yacobe!"

"I can't believe you went to so much trouble, son," Dad said. "It's been a long time ... too long ... since ..." His voice trailed off. He twisted his lips to one side.

Papa-Ben reached over and patted Dad's hand.

Cobber's cheeks went hot at their compliments, and he grinned first at Papa-Ben, then at Dad. This—*this!*—was the family-dinner-table feeling he'd imagined. He wanted to wrap himself in it like a blanket, hold tight, and not let go.

"And now the *hamotzi*," Papa-Ben said.

Cobber suffered through first Papa-Ben's then Dad's attempts to slice a piece of challah for the blessing. He bit his lip, and, all at once, his eyes felt hot and itchy.

"Never mind, Yacobe. We will use the whole thing, eh?"

He tried not to look at the stone challah while Papa-Ben said the blessing. It was a relief when Dad finally shooed him off to bring dinner.

No wonder Mrs. Berman had called it soup. The chicken had fallen off the bones, the potatoes and carrots turned to mush, and he discovered little bags of organ-looking things floating in the foaming water. He fished them out and strained the rest into the soup tureen, grateful Mrs. Berman had set it out for him. Her spaghetti stuff was starting to seem like a welcome addition to the meal.

Cobber opened the oven, pulled the rack out with a potholder, and peeled back the foil. Fat meatballs wrapped in yucky leaves bubbled in a thick, red sauce. Dotting it were little rabbit-pellet things—raisins, he assumed. He couldn't believe it. She had brought Papa-Ben's favorite—stuffed cabbage! Too bad it wasn't his as well.

Dad and Papa-Ben oohed and aahed through the salad and stuffed cabbage. At last Cobber ladled out the soup.

He stared at his bowl. Dad and Papa-Ben seemed to be waiting for him to taste it first. Maybe the chicken-potato-and-carrot mush would be more appetizing than it looked. Gingerly, he sipped a spoonful. It wasn't bad, he realized. In fact, given how hungry he was, it was great!

Dad and Papa-Ben spooned theirs up too. Papa-Ben declared it as good as Grandma's. He had devoured three whole bowls before he wiped his lips with his napkin and sighed. "What a *mensch* you are, Yacobe," Papa-Ben said. "A good and decent person, eh? I cannot tell you." His gaze held Cobber's. How he loved the way Papa-Ben looked at him, despite the challah and the mushy chicken soup!

"That's the most I've seen you eat all week, Papa," Dad said. "Oh, shoot." He glanced at his watch and rose abruptly. "We'd better get a move on, if we're going to make it to services on time."

Cobber eyed the dishes, wondering whether his job was done. It *was* a big deal, making *Shabbos*. The preparations and the clean up just went on and on. He reached for Papa-Ben's plate, but Dad shooed him away.

"I'll get those, son. You go up and change your clothes."

"You're sure?"

"Very. You did a good thing here tonight." Dad's eyes looked shiny. "You know that, don't you?"

Cobber pressed his lips together, squirmed at Dad's words. His attention.

"Your mom would be proud."

"Yeah, well," he said, "I tried."

"And succeeded." Dad ruffled his hair, then collected the dishes.

Cobber helped Papa-Ben up from his chair and turned to go. But his great-grandfather reached out, touched his cheek, and patted it softly. "A real *mensch*, you hear me?"

Cobber nodded, drowning in all the praise. It was too much. "Sorry about the challah," he said.

Papa-Ben shook his head. He was about to speak, but a choking gasp escaped instead. A moment of panic flashed in his eyes, and then he was pushing Cobber away, away with both hands, and moving—moving fast for him—down the hall. Down the hall and into the bathroom. Closing the door. And barfing, from the sound of it.

Chapter 19

"He's not going anywhere tonight," Dad said, pacing outside the bathroom. "That's for darned sure."

"I poisoned him, didn't I?" Cobber sank to the floor and pulled his knees to his chest. "I'm never going to forgive myself."

"Don't be silly. This is not your fault. Maybe he ate too fast. Come on. Get up now."

Cobber sighed and dragged himself up. He listened at the door for more signs of distress. *Please, God, let him be okay. Let it not be my fault.*

"I'm serious. There's nothing to forgive." Dad's arm weighed heavily on Cobber's shoulder. "You boiled the hell out of that chicken, son. Salmonella didn't stand a chance."

Cobber turned, sudden tears gathering in the corners of his eyes. "But why, then?"

"Who knows? He ate more than he's used to, that's for sure. And like I said before, he's old. His immune system's not the best. For all we know, he could have picked up some kind of bug at the doctor's."

Cobber's lip wobbled. He tried to bite it into stillness. "You think?"

"I know."

All night they kept vigil—Dad on the sofa, Cobber in Papa-Ben's recliner. The vomiting gave way to a hoarse cough that wracked Papa-Ben's poor body more and more with each bout. By morning, he lay there, limp as a wet washrag, spent from his efforts. There was no way any of them was going to Rosh Hashanah services. But Cobber vowed to pray at home. Saturday seemed endless, with Papa-Ben unable to eat much or keep anything down. Cobber didn't have the heart to go practice any magic tricks upstairs. By dinnertime, Dad was talking about taking him back to the hospital.

"No, Larry, you listen to me now," Papa-Ben said. "No more hospitals."

"But, Papa—"

"I have a bed. I have a family. I need a hospital like a hole in the head."

"What if we can't help you?" Cobber pleaded.

"*Genug*! Enough already." Something sparked behind Papa-Ben's watery eyes. "God will help me, Yacobe. I am in His hands."

Part of Cobber hated that Papa-Ben believed that. But the other part wanted to believe it himself. Wanted to believe that God really *would* take care of Papa-Ben. Of him. Of all of them. That He was taking care of Mom even now.

Dad gave up arguing and made some calls to line up a nurse from Jewish Social Services instead of Papa-Ben's usual caregiver. An hour later, Papa-Ben's doctor called back with instructions for "keeping him comfortable."

When Dad hung up, he sank into one of the kitchen chairs, his face in his hands. Cobber wondered what was going on but was afraid to ask. Did he really want to know? At last, his father looked up again. "Sit with him, will you, son?" he said. "I-I need to go upstairs for a while."

By the time Papa-Ben finally fell asleep, Dad had not returned, so Cobber went in search of him. A strange hiccup-y sound greeted him at the top of the stairs. The door to the guest bedroom was ajar. Cobber tiptoed in. The blinds were drawn, but a light from the closet cut a swath of cream carpet and lilac bedspread. The pungent smell of cedar tickled his nose.

"Dad?" he whispered. "What are you doing in here?"

The strange sound stopped abruptly. A shuddering breath and a brisk sniff followed. Dad, crying? Cobber hesitated, not wanting to intrude. *But what if he needs me?* Swallowing hard, he approached the walk-in closet and peered inside.

Dad's back was toward him, his shoulders hunched as if Cobber had just let in a blast of wintry cold. Beyond him were hanging zippered compartments full of clothes. A splash of purple spilled out of one. Yards and yards of lacy white escaped another.

"Um." Dad cleared his throat. "Give me a minute here, son."

Cobber backed off, but his stomach started working overtime. No one went into the guest bedroom—not even guests. But maybe Dad needed something out of storage. Something for Papa-Ben. Cobber wished there were bottles or knickknacks on the dresser. He'd line them up perfectly. Space them out just so. He swiped his finger through the dust, leaving a long scar, an exclamation mark with no period.

When Dad finally turned, the dim light dragged his cheeks down like fingers. "What?" Cobber said. "Tell me."

"I'm sorry." Dad rubbed one eye for a long moment. His voice sounded gravelly, lower than usual. "This stuff with Papa-Ben." He pressed a fist to his lips and seemed to fight with himself to go on. "That beautiful *Shabbos* you made yesterday—you know, that's my first without your mother? It all got me thinking."

"About what?"

"Your mom. And the rest of us."

"And?"

"And it's time I make room, Jacob."

Cobber sucked in his breath. This had to be serious if Dad called him Jacob. "Make room for what?"

"For you. For me. For both of us." Dad's eyes glittered.

Cobber blinked up at him, swallowed hard.

"Come, look at this closet. All her things. See? This was her wedding dress." As Dad pulled it from the garment bag, it whispered of Mom's perfume and sparkled in the light. "You ever see this?"

"In pictures." Cobber fingered some tiny crystal beads that dotted the lace. "What's that purple one?"

"Her prom dress."

"Why … why do we still have all this stuff?" *No wonder I never remembered packing boxes!*

Dad shrugged. "Just couldn't make myself go through it. Let it go."

Cobber thought of the Ouija board he'd been hiding all this time under those sweaters in his own closet. Of what it meant to him. Then he thought of Mom's latest message. Maybe WN meant *when* good-bye. Maybe she was asking when *he* was going to say good-bye. "Don't you mean, let *her* go?" he said at last.

Dad nodded, hung his head. "But it's time now. Seeing you last night—really seeing *you*—I realize I need to go through all this and make room. Space."

"I could help," Cobber said. "We could do it together."

"Yeah, I think that's the way it's got to be, kiddo. You and me. Together. No matter what."

"But … but what about Papa-Ben?"

"Whatever happens, happens," Dad said. "If *he* believes he's in God's hands, well, maybe he is. Maybe we all are. I don't know."

Cobber remembered how God had answered his prayer the night Papa-Ben took those pills. "I think I'm starting to. *Know*, I mean."

"Really? I'm glad." Dad smiled. "Wish I could have been more help. I guess me and God, we're still working things out. Maybe I've got to make room for Him, too."

"Oh, Dad." Cobber pressed his lips together, but his

eyes welled, betraying him. He tried to look away, but Dad cupped his cheeks with cool hands, tipping his face up.

"Come here, you." His father opened his arms then, and Cobber rushed forward to fill the empty place between them. A whiff of something more than soap, something sweet and spicy, welcomed him. Pressing into the soft crush of Dad's velour shirt, Cobber closed his eyes against a sudden burning. He melted into the moment and just breathed.

* * * *

All through the long week, between secretive practice sessions for the talent show, Cobber sent up prayers, quick and private, for Papa-Ben. And *Thank you, God*s, too, for that connection with Dad. God willing, there would be more. Cobber smiled at the thought.

By Saturday, Papa-Ben started to rally. The paper color had left his face. He hardly ever coughed anymore, and he was eating again. Not much—canned soup mostly. But at least he was keeping it down. Best of all, he was able to get up for a while and sit in his favorite chair. Whenever Cobber saw him there, he whispered another "Thank you, God," more confident than ever now that He would hear.

There was no way, though, that Dad would let Papa-Ben go to Kol Nidre services Sunday evening. Not even using a wheelchair, if they could have gotten their hands on one.

"Okay," Papa-Ben agreed, finally. "But tomorrow, I go.

I am telling you, Larry. Yom Kippur, I will not miss. You do not take me, I call a cab."

Even though they left for temple well before ten on Monday morning, by the time Dad had maneuvered Papa-Ben inside, worshippers already filled the sanctuary and overflowed into the adjoining social hall. Considering Lake Tilton was not exactly Madison or Milwaukee, it always amazed Cobber to see the temple so full. People must have come from miles around to attend Yom Kippur services. Dark business suits, gray sweaters and skirts, college kids in black and more black—all these blended together into one depressing tone. Everyone seemed dressed for a funeral. Everyone but Cobber. His green sweater and khaki pants screamed for attention. *Not* what he wanted. But there was no turning back now, and his only sports coat barely fit anymore.

At Dad's urging, Cobber hurried ahead to stake out some seats, three on the aisle in the second-to-last row. From this far back, he could just about see the stained-glass window—the Tree of Life and the Star of David. But all he could see of the rabbi, though raised on the bimah, was Rabbi Brahms's shiny head, peeking above the crowd.

Cobber sighed. It was going to be a long morning. Hours of prayers stretched before him. Turning around in his folding chair, he smiled encouragement at Papa-Ben's halting progress up the aisle. Clinging to Dad, barely upright, Papa-Ben looked like a withered vine. If not for his cane, he would have wilted entirely long before. But he was determined to be there to ask God's forgiveness for his sins—not that Cobber thought he had any. *Where there's a will, there's a way.* He smiled, remembering his words to Mrs. Berman. That's why he'd come—for Papa-Ben. For Dad, too. To help him make sure Papa-Ben was okay. So what if all this Hebrew stuff meant nothing to Cobber?

Finally, Dad took the seat beside him, and Papa-Ben collapsed into the folding chair on the aisle. Cobber reached around his father and touched Papa-Ben's hand. It was trembling, and Papa-Ben's narrow chest was heaving, too. But all he seemed worried about was having to wear a borrowed prayer shawl. Dad, in his hurry, had left Papa-Ben's on the table at home.

The rabbi's voice crackled a welcome through the speakers. Dad opened his book, nudging Cobber to do the same.

"This is the day of awe," the rabbi read. "What are we, as we stand in Your presence, O God? A leaf in the storm, a fleeting moment in the flow of time, a whisper lost among the stars."

Cobber shivered, feeling suddenly small. He glanced at Papa-Ben. His great-grandfather's eyes were closed, his face tipped toward the ceiling.

"Help us to mend the evil of our ways, to right the heart's old wrong … Inscribe us for blessing in the Book of Life."

The Book of Life. That was the part that got to Cobber. On Rosh Hashanah the Book of Life was supposedly opened. Then he had ten days to make amends for stuff he'd done wrong. Today was the last day—the day God would decide his fate for the next year—the day the Book was finally sealed. It sounded so dumb, when he thought about it. But what if it were true? Did he really want to risk making God mad—especially after all He'd done to help Papa-Ben?

He glanced again at his great-grandfather. So far, so good. But as weak as he still was, how could he possibly sit there for long? When the rabbi said, "Please stand," would he be able to? Now Cobber had lost his place. He flipped to the right page, surprised to see ALL RISE on the very next one.

Somehow, with Dad's help, Papa-Ben managed to stand, steadying himself against Dad and the chair in front. But his back bowed painfully. Cobber held his breath until ALL ARE SEATED finally came around and Dad eased Papa-Ben back down.

"On Rosh Hashanah we reflect," the rabbi was saying.

"On Yom Kippur we consider:

Who shall live for the sake of others,

Who, dying, shall leave a heritage of life."

The words struck unexpectedly, arrows to Cobber's heart. Mom. Why couldn't *she* live for the sake of others? For *his* sake. He rubbed his nose, twitched his lips to one side. And yet, dying, she *did* leave a "heritage of life." She left *him*. And Dad. Both of them, together. Now more than before, he hoped. A family, still. He closed his eyes, trying to call up a memory, the feel of her arms, the smell of her skin. Trying, but coming up empty.

Members of the congregation began taking turns on the bimah, leading the readings in English, then Hebrew. But the words flowed past Cobber without sinking in. All he could think about was Mom. Was her spirit still alive? Mrs. Berman sure talked like it was. Maybe his mother *was* here, right now, hovering over him, or closer. In the air he breathed, in each beat of his heart.

"On Rosh Hashanah it is written,
on Yom Kippur it is sealed;
How many shall pass on, how many shall come to be;
who shall live and who shall die;
who shall see ripe old age and who shall not ..."

At the words, Cobber jerked free of his thoughts. Papa-Ben! Where was *his* name being written today? Already he had lived and seen "ripe old age." What else but death could await him? Cobber strained to see past Dad. Papa-Ben showed no reaction to the reading, but he seemed to be melting into his chair, all strength drained now from his spine.

"Dad," he whispered, pointing at Papa-Ben.

Dad eased an arm around Papa-Ben and bent forward, talking low. Papa-Ben waved one hand weakly, as if he were shooing away a pesky fly. Then he said something Cobber couldn't hear.

"He wants to try to stay until the Torah reading," Dad said.

"Do you think he'll make it?"

Dad shrugged.

"I'm going with you, then," Cobber said.

Dad shook his head. "*One* of us has to stay. You go squeeze in next to the Bermans."

"But … why?"

"Because I …" Dad hesitated, then seemed to reconsider what he was about to say. "Because it's important. For the family. I already talked to Patty. They'll bring you home."

Cobber tried to listen to the service—*for the family*—but it seemed to drone on without end. Someone's stomach rumbled nearby. Then Dad's did. Cobber bit back a grin, waiting for a whole chain reaction. That was one good thing about being only eleven; he wasn't old enough to fast on Yom Kippur.

A familiar woman's voice came then, and he strained to see who was reading. It was that Mrs. Spector lady, the one with the stiff red hair.

"Man's origin is dust," she said, her tone thin and quivery through the microphone, "and dust is his end."

Cold fingers seemed to squeeze the back of his neck. Enough talk of death. It was giving him the creeps. Yet Papa-Ben just sat there, listening—the silent, knowing fisherman again—like the idea of dying didn't even faze him. Cobber thought if he were that old and frail, he'd be crying his eyes out by now.

Papa-Ben didn't make it until the Torah reading. Not even close. When Dad led him from the sanctuary, Cobber followed gratefully, glad for a break. In the foyer he noticed a wheelchair just sitting there, unused. It looked like it belonged to some rental company. Even so, Papa-Ben was not in favor of borrowing it, even for a few minutes, to get to the car.

"I'll stay right here," Cobber promised, "in case anyone comes looking for it."

"But it is not mine, Yacobe. How can I sin, today of all days?"

"If God didn't want you to use it, why would it be here?" he argued. "I'm telling you, Papa-Ben. Whoever brought it, he'll be doing you a mitzvah and he doesn't even know it."

Dad pressed his lips together, trying to stifle a grin, while Papa-Ben shook his head. "What can I say, Larry? The boy is a regular genius, I tell you."

Though he had promised to go sit with the Bermans after Dad left with Papa-Ben in the borrowed wheelchair, Cobber lingered in the lobby instead. All the memorial lamps blazing against the bronze-cast Yahrzeit tablets caught his eye. He searched out his mother's. The only other time hers was lit was in June, on the anniversary of her death. Slowly, he traced the raised letters of her name—BETH COHEN STERN. Then, on a crazy impulse, he twisted the bulb, snuffing out the light. He couldn't stop himself and kept repeating the action. On, off. On, off. Like her life. Is that what we all are, he wondered. Little lights for God to turn off when He feels like it?

He blinked quickly, but could not look away. He didn't know how long he stood there, staring at Mom's darkened lamp. He found no comfort there, no hope that any part of her still burned. And yet *something* did. He could feel her, even now, inside him. In the present tense. And so, finally, he twisted the bulb one last time, rekindling her name, before going back inside to sit with the Bermans.

Chapter 20

Rabbi Brahms surprised Cobber by calling that evening after Break Fast to check on Papa-Ben. He wanted to know whether it was okay to stop by later in the week for a visit.

"Can you imagine, Yacobe, the rabbi coming here? To see *me*?" Papa-Ben, propped up in bed with four pillows, wagged his head from side to side.

"I guess that's one more reason you should take it easy and get your strength back." Cobber set his Houdini book aside. Though he'd intended to read to Papa-Ben, talking was definitely easier. "You want to see my magic tricks? I-I promised a friend I'd do some in the talent show. But don't tell Dad, okay? I want to surprise him." His stomach flip-flopped just talking about it. But he wasn't sure whether it was because of stage fright or Megan.

"Maybe later, Yacobe. When is the show?"

"The twenty-seventh, right before Halloween. I hope you'll come. Dad, too."

"I hope so, too. But, Yacobe, you never know ..." Papa-Ben's voice trailed off.

Cobber nodded, unsure what to say next.

Papa-Ben sighed. "Be a good boy now and do your studies."

"But—"

"*Tschut, tschut.*" A trace of Papa-Ben's old spark danced in his eyes. "You are still going to teach me to read, eh? I only want you should be ready."

Papa-Ben announced that *he* was ready on Thursday, when Cobber came home from school. The caregiver had come earlier and gotten him washed and dressed. In his flannel plaid shirt and shiny brown pants, his stubble freshly shaven, he looked like a guy ready at last to go back to school and tackle English.

Cobber grabbed a fresh notebook, three newly sharpened pencils, and one of his favorite picture books. Mom had read *Goodnight Moon* to him every night at bedtime until he could read it himself, from memory. Maybe Papa-Ben would like it, too. All *he* brought to the kitchen table was his prayer book.

"Okay." Cobber licked his lips, suddenly nervous. What did *he* know about teaching English? "In the beginning ..."

"Ah, Genesis. Chapter one." Papa-Ben chuckled.

"Okay, class. Settle down now," Cobber teased back. "I think first we should learn the alphabet, and what sound each letter makes."

Papa-Ben nodded. "In Hebrew, too."

Positioning a blank page between them, Cobber wrote a capital and small A. Then he had Papa-Ben say the name and make the sound. Next to it, after considerable effort, Papa-Ben made a squiggly letter that looked sort of like a fancy X or maybe even a capital N. "What's that?" Cobber asked.

"You made your first letter, yes? So I made mine, too." He called it *aleph* and said it made no sound at all.

Cobber wondered why they even bothered with it, then, but he said nothing. It was one less sound he'd have to remember. A, *aleph*. So far, so good. "One down, twenty-five to go," he said.

Papa-Ben shook his head. "Yacobe, you are in luck. There are only *twenty-one* to go."

"You're kidding." He guessed Papa-Ben was going to get the worst end of *this* deal!

"What? Already, you are giving up?"

"No, are you?" He grabbed a pencil, wrote B, and had Papa-Ben make its sound.

"Aha! Like in my name. Benjamin. In Hebrew, we call it *bayz*. No, *bet*. I think that is how Boolkie learns it now." Papa-Ben had a hard time drawing this one. Maybe it was supposed to look like a backwards capital L or a sideways U, with a dot in the middle, but it was hard to tell.

"What if you showed me one in your prayer book?" Cobber suggested, not wanting to make Papa-Ben feel bad about his handwriting.

He flipped to a page with the Kiddush, and there it was, along with some little mark beneath it, in the word that meant *blessed*.

Cool. *Aleph, bet.* If the next letter was anything like C, this was going to be easy.

He wished.

The third Hebrew letter turned out to be called *gimel*, followed by *dalet* and *he*. The whole thing was as mixed up as alphabet soup. Judging by the extra furrows in Papa-Ben's forehead, he wasn't finding the going any easier in English.

"I don't know," Cobber said. "Maybe I'm not such a great teacher."

Papa-Ben grunted. "You? What about me?"

Neither of them spoke for a long, awkward moment. Cobber tried on the idea of giving up. Failing. He couldn't remember ever having caved in so quickly before. But not learning Hebrew wasn't the end of the world, was it? Look how long Papa-Ben had survived, not knowing how to read English. And that was the language of the country he *lived* in. Finally, Cobber shrugged and said, "Maybe that's enough for today. You can't say we didn't try, right?"

Papa-Ben nodded glumly. "There is something to be said for learning when you are young, eh, Yacobe?"

"You can say that again."

"Oh, like you are such an old man, eh? Listen to me, Yacobe. It is not too late to get a *real* Hebrew teacher. Have a bar mitzvah. Something special for my social calendar."

Even if he *could* learn Hebrew in what remained of Papa-Ben's life, how would he ever get up in front of all those people and make a speech? Maybe pure stubbornness *did* keep him from going with Boolkie. But now it came down to plain old stage fright and lack of confidence. Something, he realized now, he was going to have to deal with at the talent show, too, now that he'd promised Megan. "I-I'll think about it, Papa-Ben," he said finally. "I promise." It startled him how often he'd been making promises lately.

The doorbell rang then. Cobber wasn't all that surprised to see Rabbi Brahms on the front porch, and invited him in. "You saved us both," he said. "You got here just in the nick of time."

"I don't know what I saved you from, but I'm glad to be of service." The rabbi's smile set Cobber instantly at ease.

For a moment, though, he debated where to take him Papa-Ben's room? The kitchen?—but finally decided on the living room, since it had always been reserved for special company. "Papa-Ben," he called, "it's Rabbi Brahms!"

With one hand on his cane and the other on the wall, Papa-Ben slowly made his way down the hall. "It is so good of you to come, Rabbi," he said, sinking at last into a deep round chair opposite the rabbi's.

Cobber stood in the doorway, unsure whether he was supposed to be part of this.

"I just wanted to see how you were doing, Ben. I hope I'm not interrupting anything."

"No, you're not," Cobber said, too quickly, and Papa-Ben's sly wink reassured him that the so-called lessons would remain their little secret.

"Forgive me," Papa-Ben said. "Would you like some tea?"

"No, thanks." The rabbi touched the lip of a huge conch

shell that lay before him on the coffee table. "Say, while I'm here, I ought to get your parents' names, Ben. For your aliyah." He pulled out a small computer gadget from his shirt pocket and readied the stylus for taking notes.

Cobber eased into the room, and finally got up the nerve to sit on the gold velvet sofa, wearing plain old everyday jeans.

"My father was Moishe," Papa-Ben said, "and my mother was Rivka."

"Got it." The rabbi turned to Cobber. "And how are things going for *you*, Jacob?"

He shrugged.

"Well, it looks like you've been taking good care of your great-grandfather, that's for sure," he said, then faced Papa-Ben again. "I must say, you look a lot stronger. I'm glad to see it."

"Me, too. I have a talent show *and* a bar mitzvah to go to, eh?" Papa-Ben winked at Cobber. Oh, great. He had to bring that up. Cobber had promised he'd *think* about the bar mitzvah. Now the rabbi would be on his case, too.

"A talent show, huh?"

"I'm just doing a few magic tricks, that's all. It's not a big deal."

"Good for you, Jacob." The rabbi turned to Papa-Ben. "You've still got a few weeks till the bar mitzvah. Don't forget to save some energy for that." Dummy, they were talking about Eli's.

"Do not worry. I will be there," Papa-Ben said. "I

remember when I had *my* bar mitzvah. Times were different then. Not like now. A little honey cake, a little wine. And a looooong speech in Yiddish. That, they called a bar mitzvah."

"Yeah, and now it's nothing but a big show," Cobber blurted. Whoa. Where did that come from? TV? "I-I'm sorry," he mumbled. "I don't know why I said that."

"Well, it's true, sometimes," the rabbi said. "No need to apologize. I've seen a few real productions, all right. When it comes to their kids, some parents can get downright carried away."

Cobber nodded, appreciating the rabbi's kindness in giving him a way out.

"The funny thing is," Rabbi Brahms continued, "and most people don't realize this, there's not a word about bar mitzvah in the Torah. In the Talmud, yes, but not as a celebration. It was a way of obligating a person to *mitzvot.*"

Cobber's eyes went wide. Doing good deeds? Was that all it was? "Are you kidding me?"

The rabbi raised his right hand, as if he were swearing on a stack of Bibles. "I kid you not. A Jewish boy automatically becomes a bar mitzvah on his thirteenth birthday."

"Automatically? No way!" He glanced at Papa-Ben. "You mean, you don't *have* to do the ceremony, make a speech, and all that other stuff?"

Papa-Ben tipped his head from side to side. "It would be nice, Yacobe."

"Yeah, but …" He was still reeling from the rabbi's words.

"Really, Jacob, it's about taking your place as an adult in

the Jewish community," the rabbi explained, "so you can count toward the *minyan*."

Cobber frowned, and Papa-Ben jumped in, exasperated. "A *minyan*, Yacobe! Ten adults. What we need for a service. Do you *sleep* in Sunday school?"

"I-I guess I must." Cobber squirmed on the deep gold sofa cushion, trying to make sense of things. He was beginning to wish he *had* paid more attention in class. It would definitely save him some embarrassment. "But I don't get it. Who even started the whole bar mitzvah thing, then? Where did it come from?"

"In its earliest form, bar mitzvah—or these days, bat mitzvah, for girls—was a young person's first aliyah. All you had to do was come up and recite the blessing over the weekly Torah reading."

"That's it? That's all?"

"I tried to tell you before, in my office, but …"

"Sorry." His cheeks heated up with the memory of how he'd bolted from the rabbi's office and headed for Papa-Ben's. "Well, at least I know now. Thanks, Rabbi. I'm not kidding, either." *Oh, God, thank you, too!*

Chapter 21

The night of the talent show, Cobber had just loaded the last of his props into Dad's car trunk when the phone rang. He jumped to answer it, secretly hoping the talent show had been canceled. It was the only way he could get out of this now and still save face.

"Jacob, hi. It's me, Megan."

He sucked a quick breath, trying to calm his galloping heartbeat. "Hey. Hey, Megan," he managed.

"I just wanted to tell you…" Her voice trailed off. "I mean, I can't wait to see your magic tonight. I'm really glad you're doing it."

"Yeah, me too." He hoped he sounded convincing.

"What are you wearing?"

"Um, pants? A shirt? A jacket, if it still fits."

Megan's laugh tickled his ear, sent goose bumps down his neck. "No, silly. What *color*?"

"Oh, uh, a blue tie."

"Royal or robin's egg?"

"Royal, I guess. Why?"

"I want to wear the same color, so we can be connected. Energetically."

"Great." Cobber bobbed his head. He hadn't heard about an energy connection, but maybe it was similar to the spiritual connection he felt with Mom.

"Am I too late to remind you not to eat dinner?"

"Nope. I didn't."

"Good. And remember to keep going no matter what. If something goes wrong, make us laugh *with* you."

"With me?"

"Yes. People can't laugh *at* you if they are *with* you, right?"

"I-I never thought of that. Boolkie's pretty much got that sewn up, hasn't he?"

"Uh-huh. So just channel him, Jacob, and you'll be okay. I promise. And if all else fails, remember: Imagine the audience sitting there in their underpants."

Cobber laughed. "Yeah, I'll remember."

"Can't hurt, right?"

Her last words to him—"Break a leg"—echoed in his mind as he helped Papa-Ben into the car. Surely she didn't want him to do *that*, though it *would* get him out of performing.

"So your friend Megan," Papa-Ben began, "she called to wish you luck?"

"I don't know, exactly. She said 'break a leg.'"

Why were Dad and Papa-Ben both trying not to laugh?

"What?" he demanded.

"Cobber, 'break a leg' *means* good luck to performers," Dad said. "Some people think it jinxes you to say 'good luck.'"

"Oh. Nice. Then, yes, I guess she did."

"What's all that stuff you had me load?" Dad asked. "I had to rearrange a bunch of apartment things to make room."

"It's a surprise," Cobber said. And a bigger surprise if I make it through without freezing—or worse.

Dad glanced at him in the rearview mirror, but didn't press for an explanation. Cobber settled into the back seat and closed his eyes for the rest of the ride. Maybe he was praying. Or maybe he was just imagining how he wanted everything to go. Imagining he *could* rather than he *couldn't.* He tried not to obsess about the necktie that was threatening to strangle him or the sports coat that pulled across his back. He checked his left wrist to make sure he hadn't forgotten his watch. He'd need it for one of his tricks.

By the time Dad had seated Papa-Ben in the first row near the aisle and carried all Cobber's props backstage, Cobber's stomach was working overtime. From hunger— or fear? He wasn't sure. But he was glad for Megan's advice not to eat anything before the show. Now he peeked out from behind the backstage curtain, watching the middle school auditorium fill with all ages of kids, parents, and grandparents, too. He wondered if he was the only one with a great-grandparent in the audience.

The delicious scent of freshly popped kettle corn wafted from Joey's dad's Kettle Heroes booth at the back of the room. Cobber's mouth watered, remembering when Joey had brought mini-bags of it with their team logo for soccer treats. It looked like the PTA had gone all out to make the talent show festive. Green and gold crepe paper bunting hung in scallops beneath the ceiling. Someone was even pumping balloons with helium and handing them out to the little kids.

Other performers were crowding around backstage. One girl was trying to tune her cello but having a hard time hearing. A seventh grader he knew from soccer kept exercising his fingers in mid-air, then cracking his knuckles in turn. Cobber focused his attention on his setup—the little covered table he'd brought and the basket of props for his tricks. His gaze fell on a small empty silver bucket. What was that doing in there? It looked like the one Dad used to sprinkle salt on icy sidewalks at his apartments. Jeez. What was he going to do with *that*?

Finally, the announcer introduced the first act. A third grader who could have been a candidate for Little Miss America strutted onstage, wearing sequins and spangles. All curly blonde hair and lipsticked smiles, she tapped around in circles and ended with a grand *ta-da* gesture. As ridiculous as she looked to Cobber, he realized that everyone was applauding. She seemed to be bursting with pride.

He tried to concentrate on his own act instead of comparing it to everyone else's. He'd memorized the order, but that patter—ah, that was another thing. He remembered Megan's advice: make them laugh *with* you. How was he going to do *that*?

All at once, someone was pushing him toward the stage. "Cobber! Pssst! You're up!"

"Ladies and gentlemen, boys and girls, I now present the Great Cobberini!" The announcer's voice boomed through the mic. Hustling over, he helped Cobber pull the covered stand into place, nudged the prop basket toward him, and set the mic stand in front of the table.

Cobber blinked at the crowd, swallowed hard. He pulled the mic closer. Was he imagining it or was his heartbeat pounding out of his chest and through the speakers? Could everyone else hear it? He blew out a quick breath, then another. Taking Megan's last advice, he tried to imagine the audience in their underpants and bit back a grin.

Say something! Do something! His gaze wandered to his props basket and locked on the small silver bucket. He had to break the ice, had to make them laugh. A glimpse of blue in the front row pulled his focus, and he let his eyes connect with Megan's. She smiled, nodded encouragement. Even from onstage, he could see her dimples. *You've got this, Jacob!* she seemed to say.

He looked at the stupid silver bucket again, then leaned over, picked it up, and, with a flourish, set it on the table.

"The *Great* Cobberini? I don't know," he said, words finally coming. "Some of you have known me since third grade and might have your doubts. But never fear. I haven't eaten any dinner, and if I get too nervous, this magic bucket will make everything … disappear!"

He held his breath, waiting to see whether he'd already bombed. But everyone was laughing and hooting. Laughing *with* him, he realized. Out of the corner of his eye he caught Megan covering her mouth with one hand and then tipping it in his direction. He could feel his cheeks flush, his face exploding into a wide grin. Papa-Ben was clapping, and Dad was shaking his head—in amazement, Cobber realized, not disapproval.

"Seriously," he said, "for my first trick, I will show you a page from the newspaper." He held up the front page of that morning's *State Journal* and presented both sides to the audience. "I've been looking for a little gift—a silk scarf maybe. I saw an ad for one just this morning. But I don't feel like shopping. You know, when you're a magician, you can just make stuff … appear!" As he held the newspaper high with his left hand, his right seemed to pull a red scarf out of the center of the paper.

The audience drew an audible gasp, then applauded wildly. A rush of gratitude swelled Cobber's chest. He hadn't expected that reaction, that expression of awe. Flicking the scarf aside, he put the newspaper back in his basket. Now his heart was thrumming in his ears, but not from fear, he realized. From excitement.

Next he held up an ordinary piece of paper and a pair of scissors. "This is plain old copy paper, do you agree?" The crowd murmured yes. "And now I ask you all, do you think I can cut a hole big enough to walk through?"

The audience mumbled a collective no, as Cobber folded the paper and set about cutting it the same way he'd done that day for Boolkie. He sneaked a look at Dad and Papa-Ben, ultimately locking eyes with Megan. Her smile melted him. He had to look away. He wondered where Boolkie and the Bermans were. Hadn't seen them come in.

"And now," he said, "let's see who is right—you or me." With that, he held up the paper, fully expecting to be able to walk through it. But instead, it was a long mess of zig-zagging snips. "We-e-ell," he said, heat flooding his cheeks, "looks like *you're* right. No hole here, as you can see."

"Do it again," someone yelled from the back of the room. Was it a heckler? Cobber strained to see. No, it was Boolkie! "I bet you *can* do it!"

Cobber remembered a fundamental rule of magic—never repeat a trick. But he knew he'd lost concentration. This was a chance to prove himself, and Boolkie was teeing it right up. Thank goodness he'd brought extra paper.

"My bad," Cobber admitted. "A magician must always maintain focus, and I confess: For a minute there, I lost it, looking at my dad and my great-grandfather and … and my blue energy friend in the front row." His smile encompassed all three. "So I shall now prove that I *can* walk through a hole in this paper."

With that, he snipped this way and that, concentrating all the while. At last he held up a perfect circle of paper that he easily walked through. People didn't just clap. They cheered.

Buoyed now, Cobber completed the rest of his set as he'd practiced. The magic pencil that clung to the back of his open hand. The drifting ketchup packet in the bottle of water, during which he snapped his fingers and drew attention to the packet's movements with his right hand as Boolkie had coached him. Starburst candies disappearing between two blue paper plates. On an impulse, he tossed the ones that remained into the audience. Kids scrambled to catch them.

"And for my last trick, I will multiply coins in a library book." He caught the eye of Mrs. Chlapowski, the librarian, who was standing along the wall. "This should help pay my fine for that overdue magic book, right?"

"It's on me," she hollered back.

Cobber opened a fat hardcover book and dramatically placed three shiny pennies on one page. He showed it to the audience, careful not to let the pennies slide off. "And now …" He slapped the book closed and made a mysterious gesture over the cover. Then he tipped the book sideways and a whole handful of pennies sprinkled out. Opening the book again, he counted them out on the page. "One. Two. Three. Four. Five …" He stopped counting at the ninth penny.

While everyone cheered and applauded, he took a bow. His cheeks flushed as the roar continued.

"The Great Cobberini!" the announcer boomed.

As if in a fog, Cobber somehow got his props and table offstage, so the cellist could move into the spotlight. He hardly remembered gathering all his things. When he looked up, Boolkie and Megan were there, clapping him on the back and congratulating him.

"Man, Cobber, you killed it!" Boolkie said. "Even when you messed up, you managed to fix it."

"Yeah, thanks to you." Cobber grinned.

"Blue energy!" Megan said. "What did I tell you, Jacob? You were brilliant with that bucket. Just perfect."

Boolkie shook his head. "I can't believe you, man. You were so cool. I was kind of worried there for a minute."

"You weren't the only one." Cobber laughed. "But once I realized I was actually having fun, everything changed. It's like … I don't know … I just didn't care *what* people thought."

Boolkie slapped him five.

Rocking back on her heels, Megan peeked at him from beneath her eyelashes. "So, how do you feel, Jacob? I mean, really."

Awesome? Grateful? Relieved? He tried them all on before blurting, "Hungry! Anyone up for a pizza? Bet you anything my dad will buy."

Chapter 22

In the week after the talent show, Papa-Ben seemed to grow stronger every day. Cobber looked forward to being with him after school. Sometimes he would read his Houdini book aloud or they'd play checkers or cards the way they used to back at the apartment. Papa-Ben had taken to teasing Cobber about Megan's phone calls, too. "You better watch out for the young ladies, Yacobe," he'd say. "I am telling you. They will bring you nothing but *tsuris*."

"I'm not marrying her, Papa-Ben. We're just talking, that's all." He wasn't about to let on how much her phone call had helped him before the talent show and that he'd grown to like how she said *Jacob*—all sweet and slow and breathy.

Papa-Ben wasn't the only one to notice. Dad and Boolkie had, too. By the day of Eli's bar mitzvah, Cobber had a new reason to feel nervous. Megan O'Brien.

That morning Cobber, Dad, and Papa-Ben arrived at the temple way early. Papa-Ben wanted to make sure to get a seat close to the bimah. That way he wouldn't have to walk too far when they called him up to the Torah. Cobber didn't mind sitting in front either. At least today he'd be able to see. He had hoped to spend the extra time before services hanging out with Boolkie, but the Bermans were already in the sanctuary, posing for pictures—video *and* the regular kind. With all the lights and tripods, it looked like Eli was getting *married*.

Out in the lobby, Papa-Ben was clutching his blue velvet bag, the one Dad had forgotten on Yom Kippur. "Yacobe, please," he said, unzipping it. "Help me with my *tallit*."

Carefully, he withdrew a silky white prayer shawl with pale blue stripes and long fringe at each end. A shiny white yarmulke remained in the bag. "Don't you have one of these, Dad?" Cobber asked.

"Uh, yeah, I do." He shifted his weight, plainly uncomfortable at the question. "It's somewhere in that room with all your mom's things."

"But I thought you—"

"I just haven't found it yet. But I will. I'm working on it. Baby steps, son."

"Yeah." Cobber smiled, glad those steps were starting to finally bring them closer. Dad had actually told a client the night of the talent show that he was busy, he'd call her back the next day. And that was without even knowing what kind of talent Cobber planned to perform. Dad seemed to be changing *his* attitude, too.

"Yacobe, if you please?" Papa-Ben gestured to the prayer shawl.

"Oh, yeah. Sorry." He draped it around Papa-Ben's shoulders, sloped and thin despite the padding in his suit coat. "There," he said. "Perfect."

Boolkie came bounding out then, giddy with relief at being released by the photographers. "Hey, Cobber, Papa-Ben, Mr. Stern. Can you believe all the cameras? I feel like I'm on MTV or something."

Cobber laughed, but Papa-Ben shook his head. "Cameras on *Shabbat*," he said, and made a *tsk*ing sound. "You would never find that in *my* old *shul*."

Boolkie shrugged. "Well, Reform is all we've got. Take it or leave it."

"What can I say?" Papa-Ben shrugged. "Times are changing." He took the skullcap out of his little bag.

"Here, let me," Boolkie said, centering it over Papa-Ben's bald spot. "Hey. You know the definition of a yarmulke?"

"Brace yourself," Cobber said. "There's no stopping him."

"Tell me, Boolkie. What is a yarmulke?"

"A Jewish hair transplant." Boolkie pretended to play a rim shot on the drums.

Cobber grinned. Dad gave an appreciative smirk, but Papa-Ben shook his head. "Ah, Boolkie, why should today be different from any other day, eh?"

At last Dad ushered them into the sanctuary. Mrs. Berman motioned them to sit across the aisle, at the end of the second row. Dad slid in first, then Cobber, leaving the outside seat for Papa-Ben.

After he sat down, the first thing Cobber noticed—smack

dab in the center of the bimah in front of the Torah-reading desk—was a huge rainbow decoration made all of flowers. Red orange yellow green blue indigo violet. ROY G BIV, just like he'd learned in science. Was *this* the rainbow Eli had been talking about? Flowers? Big whoop.

"You like the arrangement?" Mrs. Berman swept over in a pale blue dress that swished about her knees. "I'm so happy with the way it turned out." She started rattling off names of all the flowers—orange lilies, yellow gerberas, green ti leaves, blue iris, lavender spider mums—but all Cobber focused on were the tulips, like jewels, sparkling shades of red and purple at either end of the rainbow. They reminded him of the bulbs he and Papa-Ben had replanted in the backyard. Would any of them bloom come spring? Would Papa-Ben still be here to see them?

"Cobber?" Mrs. Berman snapped her fingers to get his attention. "What do you think?"

"You mean the flowers? They're awesome," he said, trying to forget everything those tulips brought to mind. "I just wish I knew what's so great about rainbows."

"Eli will explain everything in his speech," she said, "when he talks about Noah and the ark."

She turned then to greet her relatives who kept arriving in waves, filling the rows behind Cobber and the Bermans. They were a kissy bunch, and already Boolkie's cheeks were smeared with lipstick. Cobber tried without success to catch a glimpse of Megan.

At exactly ten o'clock, Rabbi Brahms appeared behind

the reading desk. "*Shabbat Shalom* to everyone." His voice reached out like a hug. "We are so happy you are here to worship with us this morning and to celebrate the bar mitzvah of Elijah Berman."

Papa-Ben leaned toward Cobber and pointed to the bimah. "You listen," he said. "You learn."

Cobber nodded. For once, though, he felt no pressure from Papa-Ben's comment. After what the rabbi had told him about bar mitzvahs, he was finally able to stop comparing himself to Eli and Boolkie. He'd reach Jewish adulthood his own way, thank you very much. Automatically. All he cared about now was Papa-Ben's aliyah. He just hoped his great-grandfather would be strong enough.

"When a young man becomes a bar mitzvah," Rabbi Brahms was saying, "he is given the honor and the responsibility of wearing a *tallit*, a prayer shawl. It is a symbol that he accepts his responsibilities as a Jew, and a sign of the bond of love between God and His people. It is with great joy that I call Eli's father, Nate, to this pulpit—where thirty years ago he himself became a bar mitzvah—to present Eli with his *tallit*."

Cobber glanced at Dad and wondered if he was thinking about his own bar mitzvah, about Grandpa Stern giving him his *tallit*. Deep down, would he miss not giving one to *his* son?

When Eli and Mr. Berman met behind the reading desk, Eli's face was a weird scrubbed-white color, like he was going to faint or be sick. Cobber stifled a grin. He should have brought Eli that small silver bucket from the talent show. Still, he had to admit that Eli's double-breasted suit *did* make him look almost manly, and pretty much made up for his brand-new, *very* short haircut.

Mr. Berman held out a rainbow-striped *tallit*, as different from Papa-Ben's as color TV and black-and-white. It had a strip of gold writing on one edge, and Mr. Berman kissed it before placing it around Eli's neck. Then he said a prayer and gave Eli a big hug, right there in front of everybody. At that moment, Dad reached over and patted Cobber's hand.

He smiled shyly at his father, wishing he could read Dad's thoughts.

The rabbi faded off to one side then and took a seat. Mr. Berman sat down again, too, and Eli was left there, staring out with wide, dark eyes. Cobber's spit dried up just looking at him. But he supposed he'd looked that way, too, at the start of his magic act.

"Please turn to page three sixty-four," Eli said at last in a pinched, thin voice. Little by little, however, as he led the congregation in English and Hebrew readings, his voice got stronger and the pasty color disappeared.

Whenever Eli read Hebrew, Papa-Ben's lips moved silently. Cobber, on the other hand, was glad when they finally got around to the English, where the worshippers and Eli took turns. With these sections, he piped up confidently. Swept along by the rhythm of the words and the power of the voices around him, he was glad to understand the reading.

Dad strained to see past Cobber. "How's he doing?" he asked, finally.

Papa-Ben? Shoot. Had to keep an eye on him. Not let the bar mitzvah distract him.

"Please check, will you?"

Cobber nodded, closing the prayer book, while holding his place with one finger. "Papa-Ben," he whispered, "are you okay?"

"*Tschut, tschut.*" Papa-Ben's eyes flashed behind his thick glasses. He pointed toward Eli, nodded his chin. Eli was telling them to please rise. "Help me up, Yacobe."

Cobber reached around Papa-Ben, pulling him to his feet. His great-grandfather teetered for an instant, while Cobber bent down for his cane. "There. Better?" Cobber asked.

"Stop worrying, Yacobe. I am fine."

Are you really? Cobber sighed. Even if Papa-Ben were about to keel over, he'd never admit it. He was stubborn, all right. Maybe it ran in the family. Once his aliyah was over, though, they could relax. All Eli had to do was take the Torah from the Ark and they'd be home free. Wrinkling his nose at the scent of lilies wafting off the bimah, Cobber hoped he wouldn't sneeze.

Eli's voice droned on. "Elohay Avraham, elohay Yitchak, V'elohay Ya-a-kov …"

Cobber started at the sound of his name booming through the speakers. Maybe Eli was reading something about the forefathers. Cobber fumbled to find his place again, then hurried through the English translation. Strangely, there was no mention of Jacob—only Abraham and "his children" who were called to bear witness to God's glory. What was up with that?

He nudged Papa-Ben. "I heard my name," he whispered.

Papa-Ben nodded. "God of Abraham, Isaac, and Jacob, we always read. God of all generations." He pointed out four Hebrew letters in the prayer book. "That is your name."

Cobber stared, slack-jawed. Imagine that. Jacob—and with one less symbol than in English! It amazed him to think—to *realize*—that Jews had been calling his name for thousands and thousands of years, from bimahs all around the world—England, France, India, Ethiopia, and more. And yet he was hearing it—*really* hearing it—only now. Jacob. The first name his mother had given him. His grandfather's name, too. A name that sounded new and wonderful when Megan said it.

Jacob. He smiled, trying it on for size as if for the first time. No matter how he spelled it—with four letters or five—it seemed to fit just right. Like he'd finally made space for it.

Chapter 23

Jacob listened with new ears when Eli switched from Hebrew to English. *How filled with awe is this place,* Eli read, *and we did not know it!* Yes! Exactly! Though the reading went on, Jacob was too excited by his discoveries to take anything else in. Had he ever really *been* here before? Was he simply too angry at God to let himself hear?

At last Eli said, "Please be seated."

Papa-Ben sank to the pew all of one motion. Silently, Jacob cursed himself for not having watched him closer. He could have missed his seat. Fallen. And where was Jacob? Off in La-La Land, thinking about his name and this place. He had to be more alert, had to make sure Papa-Ben really *was* all right. This aliyah meant everything to him.

Dad tapped his hand. "The Torah service is coming up soon, right after the meditation," he whispered. "I hope he'll be able to make it by himself."

Jacob glanced up the aisle to the bimah. The distance had seemed so short when they first sat down. Now, looking at Papa-Ben, his *tallit* swimming about his frail body, the three steps up to the Torah seemed more like hurdles. "Yeah," he said. "Me too."

Papa-Ben closed his eyes during the meditation. He moved his lips silently and kept nodding his head. Jacob looked closer to make sure he wasn't really dozing off. So far, so good. He just seemed to be praying.

"Please rise," Eli said. Then he left the pulpit and went with the rabbi to stand in front of the Ark. His grandparents and parents joined them there. Rabbi Brahms parted the polished wood doors and drew aside a shimmering screen. Inside were three Torahs—two large and one small. He hefted out one of the big ones. Silver bells clattered from tall crowns. The fancy brown covering reminded Jacob of Papa-Ben's *tallit* bag.

"The Torah is our heritage," Rabbi Brahms said, "given by God and transferred to the elders of Israel from generation to generation. We hold it tightly as it gives us guidance, inspiration, and direction in life.

"Becoming a bar mitzvah means accepting this heritage, and, as a symbolic representation, we present the Torah now, first to Eli's grandparents, then to his parents, and finally to him, as he himself holds it and accepts the responsibility of Jewish adulthood."

As the Torah was handed from one generation to the next, Papa-Ben tensed. Was he afraid someone might drop it—or just nervous about his aliyah? Boolkie's mom strained mightily and quickly passed the Torah on to Eli. He, too, reeled under its weight, stepping backwards into the rabbi.

Jacob tried not to grin, but he couldn't help thinking that a little weight training along with the Hebrew practice would have been a good idea. What would it be like to be up there with Dad—and Papa-Ben, too? He tried the idea on gingerly, like a fancy new suit coat. Would Uncle Bob come from Los Angeles, and Aunt Gail and her family from New York? What about Mom's sister, the foreign news correspondent he'd met only once?

No. Forget it. Stop fooling yourself. No way you're ever going to do it. Just pay attention. For Papa-Ben's sake.

Before Jacob knew what was happening, Eli had carried the Torah down the bimah steps. His grandparents, parents, and the rabbi started parading it around the sanctuary. Eli's face was getting redder by the moment. In between smiles, he blew out a couple of quick breaths, as if he were bench pressing.

When the clattering bells came closer, Papa-Ben reached out into the aisle with his *tallit* fringe. Eli slowed, grinning all the while, while Papa-Ben touched the tassel first to the Torah, then to his lips. Dad reached past Jacob with his prayer book to do the same. Dumb. Should have done that, too. Shown some respect.

When they all returned to the bimah, Eli motioned sharply to Boolkie. He and two little kids Jacob had never seen before scrambled up and began removing the silver decorations—the pointer, the breastplate, and the two noisy crowns. Boolkie turned toward him with a crown in each hand, and for an instant, moved his hips like some maraca player. Jacob bit back a grin, and seconds later, Mrs. Berman cut Boolkie off with one look.

Jacob didn't realize he'd been cracking his knuckles until Dad thumped his hand. It would have been cool, being up there with Boolkie. Eli *could* have asked him. He hung around as much as any brother did. Or used to. What was so special about those little kids, anyway?

"You may be seated," the rabbi said, after he had undressed the Torah. Then he rambled on about the portion from the Book of Genesis that he and Eli were about to read.

"It's an honor to invite a number of Eli's relatives to bless the Torah as it is read," the rabbi continued. "Our first aliyah is given to Eli's paternal grandfather." He rattled off a long name in Hebrew. Mr. Berman's father approached the pulpit.

Jacob felt Papa-Ben inch to the edge of the bench beside him. Papa-Ben nudged his cane closer with his heel.

"*Barechu et Adonai hamevorach!*" Grandpa Berman sang.

The congregation echoed another line of the blessing. Mr. Berman repeated it: *Baruch Adonai hamevorach leolam vaed!* Then he continued. Jacob had heard this melody before—at one of those monthly Sunday school services. Why hadn't it sounded haunting and beautiful then? He had no idea what the words meant, and he didn't care. It didn't matter. Nothing else seemed to, right now.

Rabbi Brahms read from the Torah, then old Mr. Berman sang the blessing-after, which sounded almost the same as the first. One by one, the rabbi invited people up for an aliyah:

both Eli's parents; Great-Aunt Pearl Jacobs from Baltimore; Uncle Harry Berman from Arizona; Grandma Ruth Bernstein from Miami; Cousin Hilda Schulman from Seattle. How many was that? Why had Rabbi Brahms forgotten Papa-Ben? Surely his great-grandfather had noticed, too.

Jacob glanced over and saw him rocking back and forth, the way he used to when he'd sing Jacob's favorite lullaby. He was fine, like he'd said before. Not a care in the world. Jacob wished he himself could relax and stop worrying.

"And for our seventh aliyah—a very close friend of the Berman family—I call Benjamin Kuper to the Torah," the rabbi said finally.

Jacob could just make out the Hebrew pronunciation of Benjamin, followed by "son of Moishe and Rivka." He bent down for Papa-Ben's cane, and their hands touched as Papa-Ben took it from him.

Papa-Ben's eyes held Jacob's for a long moment, then let go. Slowly, he eased himself up and made his way, step by careful step, toward the bimah. But his balance looked off, like an old ship with too much weight on one side. Jacob cast Dad a worried look, but his father only patted his hand. Still, Jacob noticed Dad inch forward to the edge of the bench. So Dad saw it, too. Something not right.

Step by step, by slow, mincing step, Papa-Ben advanced. Since when had he been walking this way? Jacob held his breath. The rabbi came forward to help Papa-Ben up the narrow stairs. At last, Papa-Ben steadied himself against the reading desk. Rabbi Brahms smiled encouragement.

Reaching out his *tallit* fringe, Papa-Ben first touched the opened Torah scroll and then his lips. His voice didn't quite reach the microphone when he began the blessing. "*Barechu et Adonai hamevorach!*"

Jacob strained to hear the prayer, familiar now after six repetitions. He surprised himself by echoing the next line along with the rest of the congregation.

Papa-Ben licked his lips. The loose skin at his throat rose and fell around the bump of his Adam's apple. The rabbi adjusted the mic. "*Baruch* …" Papa-Ben's amplified voice sounded raspy, his breathing, fast and shallow. He closed his eyes, drew a steadying breath. "*Baruch Adonai hame*—" The word seemed to stick. A strange choking noise came out instead.

The rabbi wrapped one arm around Papa-Ben's shoulders. The mic caught his whisper: "It's all right. Take your time."

"*Hamevorah leolaaa-aaa-aaa …*"

Papa-Ben's strangled cry echoed through the speakers. *Go! Help him!* In an instant, Jacob was on his feet.

"Hey, Cobber!" Boolkie tried to catch his arm as he hurried past on his way to the bimah. "You got the calling or what? Chill, man," he whispered hoarsely.

Jacob sensed someone behind him but kept moving. What was he going to do? *Something!* Had to do *something!* When he glanced back for an instant, he saw the parted sea of faces behind him—and Dad.

But if his father intended to stop him, he had another thing coming. Leaping the three steps, Jacob rushed to Papa-Ben's side. His heartbeat thrummed in his ears.

Papa-Ben pressed his lips together, but Jacob could see them tremble. His eyes shone and he kept blinking as if he had something in them. Tears.

Jacob slipped his arm around Papa-Ben's waist and felt the bony ribcage beneath the *tallit*. Without warning, Papa-Ben's weight shifted, and Jacob struggled to keep them both standing. And suddenly, Dad was there—Dad, like a bookend, propping Papa-Ben up from the other side.

The rabbi covered the mic and whispered something Jacob didn't understand. Was he mad? Had Jacob done something wrong? Did the rabbi want them to take Papa-Ben away?

Everyone was waiting. The Torah was, too. At the sight of the opened scroll—its ancient parchment covered with dense black writing—Jacob's breath caught. He had never seen it up close before. The story of his people stretched before him and Papa-Ben and Dad like a mysterious river with no beginning and no end. He looked again at Papa-Ben—saw how frail he seemed—and suddenly found his own voice.

"*Barechu et Adonai hamevorach!*" he sang, amazed that the words came—and only slightly off-key. *You listen, you learn.*

The congregation found its voice, too, and answered back: "*Baruch Adonai hamevorach leolam vaed!*"

Jacob echoed the same line, and this time heard Papa-Ben and Dad join in. The rest of the prayer was there on his tongue the instant he needed it, as if it had always been there, waiting for him to say it.

While the rabbi read from the Torah, Jacob glanced at his great-grandfather. Whatever had happened before, Papa-Ben seemed composed now, almost peaceful. His hand brushed Jacob's, and, for a crazy instant, Jacob thought he saw him wink.

As they warbled through the blessing-after, Papa-Ben continued to gain strength from somewhere—maybe from Jacob. Maybe from Dad as well. He seemed fine now. No doubt it was only the bar mitzvah that had choked him up—him wishing it were Jacob's instead of Eli's. Well, he'd better deal with it. Jacob had. Thanks to the rabbi.

They took the steps one by one, together, but as Dad slipped into their row, Papa-Ben whispered in Jacob's ear, "Take me out, Yacobe. I need some water. I have to take a pill."

Jacob mouthed an explanation to Dad. When he and Papa-Ben reached the door, the rabbi was calling Eli, finally, for his aliyah and reading. Shoot. The highlight of the whole thing, and now Jacob would have to miss it. At least Dad was still there.

In the lobby, Papa-Ben stopped at the water fountain and took his pill. He pointed to the upholstered bench near the door. "I need to sit down, Yacobe. Please."

Jacob held his arm. "What's the matter? Should I get Dad?"

Papa-Ben patted the cushion beside him, and Jacob sat. His great-grandfather's eyes brimmed with something he'd never seen before. "Yacobe," he said finally, "do you realize what just happened?"

"Uh, you almost keeled over?"

"No, after."

"We missed Eli's chanting?"

"No, before."

Jacob blew out a long breath. "You mean when I said the blessing?"

Papa-Ben nodded. "Never mind about Eli. You, my dear Yacobe, just had *your* first aliyah, too. Do you realize that? I did not think you could do it, but you did."

"What?" *My first aliyah? Wait. Didn't the rabbi say …?* "Papa-Ben, are you telling me … I'm a bar mitzvah?"

"Not technically. At your age, you're not really allowed to have an aliyah. But now, you can see, you are really ready for your *real* one."

Jacob sucked in a breath, realizing he had broken a rule. No wonder the rabbi seemed angry.

"*Tschut, tschut.* Do not worry. I am so proud of you, Yacobe, for helping me and saying the blessing on your own."

"You and Dad, you were both there to hear me! But … how?"

Papa-Ben shrugged. "Perhaps some plans are bigger than us, Yacobe. What can I say? But I told you listen and learn, and you did." He clapped Jacob on the back. "Congratulations, my boy!"

Jacob's cheeks, his whole body burned as the realization of what had just happened sunk deeper. All he'd been thinking about was helping Papa-Ben. How had the rest of it—worry about leading the service, people looking at him, not knowing the right words—fallen away?

"Let me rest one more minute, eh?" Papa-Ben said. "Then we will go back."

Jacob agreed, but when they opened the door at last to go inside, Eli was already giving his speech. They'd missed his chanting. Oh well. Jacob could always watch the video to see if Eli's voice held out. Worried about interrupting now, he listened from the doorway, his arm around Papa-Ben.

"There's so many things I didn't realize about Noah, until I started studying for my bar mitzvah," Eli was saying. "First, he wasn't Jewish. Second, Noah was the first environmentalist. And third, that all of us—no matter the color of our skin or where our families come from—we're all descended from *him*, from this one guy. We each are part of the same human family that was born in hope and peace after God chose Noah—one righteous man—to survive the flood. At the same time, God chose to save all kinds of animals, too, and he promised never to kill all of us off ever again. It's the least *we* can do not to kill off animals and each other with our own neglect and hatred.

"To seal His promise, God gave us the rainbow and made the bow part face away from earth. This shows that God is not aiming to destroy all of humanity. A bow could symbolize war, but the rainbow promises love and peace instead. Unfortunately, peace doesn't appear as effortlessly as a rainbow after a storm. All of us have to do our part to keep peace alive.

"For my mitzvah project, I chose to help the Humane Society and …"

Wow. Incredible. Who would have ever thought Eli Berman could write a speech like that, could think those thoughts, even? Jacob shook his head, still trying to absorb Eli's words. Animals and people on the same plane—and all because of Noah?

Papa-Ben tapped Cobber's hand. "That's your Megan, yes?" He gestured toward the back row. "The young lady there, making goo-goo eyes?"

"That's her all right." Jacob waved and smiled. Even from this distance, he could see her dimples, and his stomach rose and fell. He would definitely have to ask her to dance later at Eli's party. Maybe she'd like to learn the *horah*—one thing he *did* remember from Sunday school.

Dad must have gotten worried about them, because the next thing Jacob knew, his father was coming up the aisle. When he reached the foyer, he gently shut the door, walling out the service. "Are you two all right?" he asked.

"We are fine, Larry. I had to get a drink." Papa-Ben stood and leaned heavily on his cane.

Dad took his free arm. "We'd better get back." He turned to go.

"No, wait! I've got to tell you something, Dad. Something amazing."

Papa-Ben grinned. "Listen to this, Larry. You will never believe it."

"I broke the rules but … I just … sort of … had my first

aliyah—that's really what a bar mitzvah is, you know. The rabbi told me so himself. I never knew that before and—"

"What?" Dad pruned up his forehead.

"Don't you see? I *did* it, Dad—said the whole prayer all by myself. And you were there, and Papa-Ben was, too."

"Cobber, wow! That *is* amazing! I'm so proud of you, son. You're full of all sorts of surprises, aren't you?" Dad raised one eyebrow, though, at Papa-Ben.

"I swear to you, Larry, I did nothing. Go talk to the Chief Engineer, you should forgive the expression."

"I'm working on it, Papa." Dad kept shaking his head in disbelief. Finally, he approached a nearby rack of community prayer shawls outside the sanctuary. "I wish I could offer you one, Cobber," he said, "but as you know, technically, you're too young."

"That's okay." Jacob sidled up, caught his hand, and gave it a quick, awkward squeeze. "If you hadn't gone up there, Dad …" His voice trailed off. No way he could have held Papa-Ben up all by himself. "Just … thanks."

"No problem, kiddo."

"I swear, if Papa-Ben didn't faint, I was sure *I* was going to."

"Well, if you did, I would have caught you." Dad grinned.

"Yeah, I guess I know that. Now." He looked down, away, anywhere but in Dad's eyes.

Papa-Ben cleared his throat. "Larry, should we go in?"

"I, uh, I need to make a stop first."

Cobber expected him to get a drink or head for the bathroom. Instead, he approached the Yahrzeit board.

"Beth." Dad touched Mom's name as Jacob had done on Yom Kippur. "Our son's first aliyah," he said, and laughed. "You saw, didn't you?"

Mom, in the present tense again. Jacob's throat went dry. He stared at the now-unlit lamp. Gone but definitely not forgotten, he thought, and wrapped one arm around Dad, the other around Papa-Ben.

"Come on, men," Dad said finally. "Maybe we're not too late to say Kaddish." He took Papa-Ben's free arm once more, and Jacob let them go. "And, yes, Papa, I do remember the prayer."

Dad and Papa-Ben eased toward the door, but Jacob lingered beside the memorial tablet. They would say Kaddish for Mom, for Papa-Ben's sister and mother in that old photo, for his father and wife and children, for all generations. Maybe those words to God would make the hurting stop. For now. Could he say them, too? Was that enough? He blinked quickly, trying to focus on Mom's name. But it was a blur.

"Psst! Cobber," Dad whispered.

He pulled himself away and entered with Dad, pressing Papa-Ben between them like a memory in a book. It took forever for them to make their way to the second row. Eli didn't seem to mind, though. He was sitting off to one side with his grandpa, looking flushed but definitely relieved.

"Our thoughts turn now to those who have departed this earth," the rabbi was saying.

Jacob and his family slid into their row and remained

standing for the Kaddish. Dad's and Papa-Ben's gravely voices surrounded him in stereo, joining the others in Hebrew. "*Yitgadal veyitkadash shemei raba …*"

The words sliced through Jacob, cutting deep. He thumbed through the prayer book, trying to find the English in time, to read along himself. Trying still, but failing.

With a sigh, he inched closer to Papa-Ben and closed his eyes. The somber rumble of prayer surrounded him and sent shivers down his spine. We *are* survivors, he thought. All of us. Every person in this room. The memory of that fishing trip floated through his mind. Crazy. But wasn't it like they—Jews everywhere—were all in the same boat, bobbing along, having faith that something was out there, down there, all around, keeping them afloat? A feeling— familiar but not, like the remains of a dream—bubbled up from a strange deep place inside him, swelling his chest, warming him, filling him up. It made it hard to breathe.

"*Yisraeil, veimeru: amein,*" the mourners intoned.

Dad leaned forward. "Cobber, did you find your place?"

He thought for a moment with his heart and answered with a nod. Dad eased his arm around Jacob's shoulder and held tight. Papa-Ben's *tallit* brushed his hand. Catching hold of the fringe, Jacob felt the pull of generations back and back through time. He did not let go.

Glossary

Aliyah (ah-LEE-yah or ah-lee-YAH): literally, "going up." Considered a great honor, it most often refers to the person being called from the congregation to say the Torah blessings while the Torah is being read. Using the second (modern Hebrew) pronunciation, making aliyah refers to one or more immigrants "going up," or immigrating, to Israel. The plural is **aliyot.**

Ark: the place on the **bimah** where the Torahs are kept. A door or adorned drapery protects the holy scrolls inside. When the Ark is opened, all worshippers remain standing.

Ashkenazi (osh-ken-AH-zee): the culture of the group of Jews, who, by the Middle Ages, had settled in northern Europe—England, France, Germany, and northern Italy. Originally subject to Christian rule, these Jews were later chased eastward, as were **Sephardi** Jews from Portugal and Spain. As the Ashkenazim settled in Germany, Poland, and Russia, they adopted their own folk language, called **Yiddish.**

Bar/bat mitzvah (bar/baht MITS-vah): literally, "son/daughter of the commandments." B'nai mitzvah is the age at which a child becomes religiously responsible and is considered an adult member of the congregation. Also, the ceremony celebrating that change in status, which is usually held around the thirteenth birthday.

Bayz: the eastern European (**Ashkenazi**) name of the second letter in the Hebrew alphabet; **Sephardi** (with origins in Spain and Portugal) Jews and Modern Hebrew speakers call the same letter "Bet."

Bet: see **Bayz**.

Bimah (BEE-mah): the raised part of the sanctuary from which the Torah is read, also where the rabbi or leader of the service stands while leading the congregation.

Blintz: an Ashkenazi Jewish dish made of golden egg-based crepes; stuffed with cheese, potato, or fruit; and usually served with sour cream and powdered sugar (icing sugar).

Break Fast: the meal after sundown on Yom Kippur, when Jews gather together to officially end their day of fasting.

Challah (HAH-lah): the braided egg bread used ceremonially during Sabbath and festival dinners.

Chanukah: the Jewish Festival of Light, usually celebrated in late November or in December. It lasts for eight days and recalls the victory of the Maccabees in 167 BCE (Before the Common Era). Although it is a relatively minor holiday, Chanukah—especially in America—has become well known since Christmas is celebrated in the same season.

Erev (as in Erev Rosh Hashanah): Jewish holidays begin at sundown on the night before the common calendar lists them; the word *Erev* before a holiday's name refers to services that are held the "night before."

Fresser (Yiddish): a big eater.

Genug (ge-NOOK) (Yiddish): that's enough.

Gott (Yiddish): literally, "God."

Hamotzi (hah-MOE-tzee): the blessing over the bread that is recited before meals.

Kaddish (KAH-dish): the memorial prayer said for the dead.

Kiddush (KID-ish): the prayer that is said over the wine (or grape juice) before Sabbath and festival dinners and other special religious occasions.

Kol Nidre (kole NID-ray): the famous, ancient prayer for absolution that opens the evening service of Yom Kippur. Famous for its music, more than its words, the prayer asks God to forgive congregants for not keeping promises to Him. Only the person who has been wronged can offer forgiveness for the sins committed against him or her.

Kosher: (referring to food and places where food is eaten) meeting the requirements of Jewish dietary laws. Common ways of "keeping kosher" include not mixing milk with meat, and not eating shellfish or pork. Not all Jews choose to follow these laws. Some who do must have their meat shipped from special kosher butchers in distant cities.

Kugel (KOO-gl): a Jewish noodle pudding, often made with cinnamon, eggs, cream cheese, and applesauce. Variations in the recipe are handed down from generation to generation.

Ladino: the folk language adopted by **Sephardi** Jews, comprised of a mixture of Hebrew and Old Spanish.

Luz (Yiddish): an order to "be quiet."

Mandelbrot (MON-dell-broht): a hard, finger-shaped cookie containing nuts, similar to biscotti.

Menorah (men-NOR-uh): the ritual candle holder, especially the one used exclusively during **Chanukah**. No matter what the artistic design, the Chanukah menorah has eight branches, plus an extra for the candle used to light the others. A menorah with seven branches was used in the ancient Temple. A seven-branched menorah also stands outside the Israeli Knesset (Parliament) and is found inside **Reform** temples today. Orthodox synagogues, on the other hand, display six-branched menorahs to represent the loss of the Jerusalem Temple.

Mensch (Yiddish): a decent honorable person, someone of noble character, literally (from the German) "a human being."

Meshuggeneh (me-SHUG-en-uh) (Yiddish): The feminine form for the word "crazy." The masculine form is "messhuggener." Variations, also meaning "crazy," are "mishegoss" and "meshugge."

Mezuzah: (me-ZOO-zuh): a ritual object fastened to the doorway of Jewish homes. Usually about three inches long, the small metal, wooden, ceramic, or glass case contains a tiny parchment scroll inscribed with fifteen verses from the book of Deuteronomy (Deut. 6:4–9 and 11:13–21). The first sentence is the **Shema**, the core prayer that affirms Jewish faith in one God. The mezuzah is usually mounted about five feet from the floor at an angle, to the right of the entrance. It is a constant reminder of God's presence and a sign that the home is Jewish.

Minyan (MIN-yen): a quorum of ten Jewish adults (in Orthodox congregations, all men) traditionally required for public worship.

Mitzvah (MITS-vuh): a commandment or good deed.

Ouija board (WEE-gee, in the US. WEE-juh, in the UK): a board with letters, numbers, and other signs around its edge, to which a pointer, or upturned glass, moves, supposedly in answer to questions from people at a seance. This grew out of Americans' growing interest in spiritualism in the mid-1800s. Charles Kennard of Baltimore, MD, invented the Ouija in 1890. It is best used by two people who place their fingertips on opposite sides of a plastic or wooden device called a "planchette," then ask a question. Despite popular belief, the name Ouija does not come from the French "*oui*" and German "*ja*," both meaning "yes."

Priestly Blessing: the blessing Papa-Ben recites in Chapter 15 is a variation of what is written in Numbers 6:24–6. In it, God tells Moses what to say to Aaron and his sons, as well as the words they should use to bless the people of Israel. When a parent places hands on a child's head and utters these ancient words of blessing, that parent is using his or her holiness to ask for God's blessing upon that child. The parent, rabbi, cantor, or anyone can become a holy conduit for God's love and blessing.

Reform Judaism: the largest and fastest-growing movement of North American Jewry, it is a combination of tradition and modernity and features prayer both in English and in Hebrew. About 42 percent of American Jews are Reform. More traditional movements include Conservative (less than 40 percent) and Orthodox (less than 6 percent), among others.

Rosh Hashanah (ROSH hah-SHAH-nah): the Jewish New Year, the beginning of the High Holy Days. It usually takes place in September or early October.

Seder (SAY-der) plate: the special plate displaying the ritual foods used before the Passover meal begins.

Sephardi (suh-FAR-dee): the culture of the group of Jews who lived under Muslim rule in Spain and Portugal. These Jews were pioneers in poetry and philosophy. Expelled during the Inquisition in 1492, the Sephardim had their own folk language, **Ladino**, a mixture of Hebrew and Old Spanish.

Shabbat (shah-BOT): the Sabbath, observed by Jews from sundown on Friday night to sundown on Saturday. Its Yiddish form is "Shabbos."

Shabbat shalom: literally, "a peaceful Sabbath to you." This is the traditional greeting on the Sabbath.

Shalom (shah-LOME): peace.

Shema (shuh-MAH): the most famous of all the Hebrew prayers, it is an exclamation that affirms the belief in one God. It is considered the watchword of the Jewish people.

Shul (Shool): Derived from the German word *Schule* (school), but in Jewish usage it is a synonym for temple or synagogue.

Tallit (tah-LEET): a prayer shawl, usually presented by a father to his child on the occasion of their bar or bat mitzvah. Worn throughout their life.

Talmud (TAL-mood): the most famous collection of Jewish teaching, assembled from the third to seventh centuries CE.

Tsuris (TSUR-iss) (Yiddish): trouble or worry.

Yahrzeit (YAHR-tzite): the anniversary of the death of an immediate relative.

Yarmulke (YAH-m'l-kuh): the Yiddish word for a head covering, usually a small skullcap that is worn on the back of the head; otherwise known as a "kippah" (kee-PAH).

Yiddish (YID-ish): the language, mainly a mixture of Hebrew and German, used for 1,000 years by Jews in and from eastern Europe.

Yom Kippur (YOME kee-POOR): the Jewish Day of Atonement, which follows Rosh Hashanah, the Jewish New Year, by ten days.

Author's Note

This novel began over twenty years ago with a scribbled haiku following a conference speaker's challenge to write about "your own culture." Its ending reflected the emotions I felt on seeing the opened Torah scroll for the first time in my life at my son, Rudi's, bar mitzvah some twenty-seven years ago. What a journey it's been from the seed of an idea to a complete story! I am grateful to members of my long-time manuscript group: Patricia Curtis Pfitsch (bread baker extraordinaire, who coached me on what Cobber should do wrong), Jack Pfitsch, Stephanie Golightly Lowden, and Dale-Harriet Rogovich for critiquing drafts of this manuscript over many years' time; and especially to Michael Leventhal of Green Bean Books and to Catriella Freedman and the Harold Grinspoon Foundation for bringing *Calling Cobber* to a new generation of readers unlikely to have known a Jewish immigrant like Papa-Ben.